Agents 2

Agents 2

No Way . . . but Are We a Team?

Written by: Anushka Arvind

Illustrations by: Ipsita Pramanik

PARTRIDGE

To order additional copies of this book, contact
Partridge India
000 800 10062 62
orders.india@partridgepublishing.com

www.partridgepublishing.com/india

Contents

Acknowledgements

I would like to thank my parents, friends and relatives for their support in the writing of this book. This book is based on my imagination and it's meant for the enjoyment of all readers. It is the second of the series of three in continuation of Agents 1.

My parents supported me very much in writing stories and always answered any queries related to what I wanted to know. This book series is not connected to my previous work "The Letter and the Hit List", though some things might be coincidental. I would like to thank those who helped me in getting details right of this book, i.e., internet, maps, people, etc.

Whatever situation this book portrays, whether good or bad, is just a situation. I equally respect all types of people, culture, etc.

I also thank my publisher for their help.

I lastly thank you, the reader for your continued interest and support.

Dedications

To my friends and family...

Prologue

"Hey!!!!" the top 50 agent shouted out.

At that the target stopped limping away and turned around to face her.

I can't let her go! I must fight!

"You are not going anywhere!!" she said.

"In what state are you in to tell me that, huh?" the target calmly replied.

She was just about to turn around to go when she stopped and turned around at what the little brave agent said.

"Bring it. I'll fight you." She said.

The target laughed out loud in the shrillest voice which was atrocious to hear!

"Don't you fear for your life, kid?" she asked, in amusement.

"Nice weapon you got there." Said the agent.

"It's my creation. It can cut through anything!" she said.

"You only have your weapons to save you…or else you'd be dead." Said the agent.

"Even if that was true…my death wouldn't be by your hand!" said the target.

"Want to bet on that?" the agent taunted.

"Come on then!" – throwing her sword down – "Anytime now!" she said and took a stance.

To be continued…

Chapter One – He escaped!

At the IB Headquarters in New Delhi, an important annual all Defence branch Directors' meeting with the Board of the IB and a few advisors from the Ministry of Defence was held. Every branch Director like the LSS was also present in the room with a long conference table and a few extra chairs. Everyone assembled in the building conference hall with impatience because of their workloads but the LSS Director settled down and waited patiently for the meeting to start.

Surely the issue of Prakash will be in this one too…always talking about it won't do any good. He's crazy and dangerous! His associates are just like him!

A group of officials swiftly entered as soon as two officers opened the doors. A few gentlemen with one lady entered with folders in their hands and took their places at the long centre table indicating themselves as the main speakers. They started to organise their files, fix ties, adjust their suits, etc., as there was still time till the National Security Advisor arrives.

But what got into this guy to take over the LSS branch? Was he just taunting me? And he did not get a plastic surgery…

While recalling the incident at LOCKER 01 where she saw a board member himself tackle down Prakash, a piece of plastic shimmered from his neck and made her suspicious. She immediately touched it and pulled on it to find herself peeling a mask off!

But if he wore a mask, the agency should have realized during security scanning…or else, someone helped him from inside.

She thought while turning the ring on her finger. Just then, a tall sturdy gentleman entered with five guards in grey uniforms, each having AK – 53s strapped to themselves, and they sit down at a designated table near the speakers.

It was not ethical to share details about those people to the top 400…but I had to…I just…I have a bad feeling that he will still target there…but why? He's constantly infiltrating the Intelligence. What exactly does he want?

As they settled down in their seats, one of the Board members, a middle-aged wheatish skinned lady with brown eyes and dark brown hair neatly curled into a bun having on a formal suit, stood to address the gathering.

"Good morning to all present for the annual discussion. I thank you all for being here, especially to the National Security Advisor from the Prime Minister's Office. Now, there are various issues which I will first highlight and during each, only filed evidences will be discussed. Let's begin this open session." She announced.

Everybody became silent. She took out a clipboard having a few sheets of paper attached to it and cleared her throat again. The projector was switched on and the first picture displayed onto the screen behind the long table.

"The first main problem that needs to be addressed is regarding criminal number 1052, former agent Prakash Kapoor. He had impersonated as Varun Srinivas and had become the former Director of the IB's LSS branch and right now sitting in the Tihar jail. He had a company of arms dealing with major terrorist groups around the world. RA&W sent a few Agents to tip off places to find out about the operations conducted. They found nothing useful. There is always a chance of his associates trying to rescue him. The issue here is what to do with him. He's placed there temporarily. The supreme court is not able to proceed with the hearing due to lack of evidence of his company." She stated and sat down.

This indicated an open session.

"RA&W couldn't find anything, you say?" Said one Director, eying the representative of RA&W.

The representative ignored the Director completely.

"Letting him go is out of the question, I guess." Said another.

"Don't think of that! Last time Interpol got him! This time it was Agent Rao, current LSS Director. Good job, by the way." Said one Board member.

"Thank you, sir..." replied the LSS Director.

"Any solutions, Agent Rao? He once worked with you." Asked the Chair.

"He stays there. There is quite a difficulty in finding evidence regarding his old company but it's possible." She replied.

"Are you saying that you can do it when RA&W could not?" asked another board member.

"I'm not saying that I can do it...I'm saying that I can get people who can do it." She replied.

"Who?" everybody wondered.

Suddenly, a few board members, including the Chair received phone calls.

"Hello? WHAT?!...How can you let this happen?!...Did you send word out? Okay good…update me later!" she said and cut the call.

"I'm very sorry but the meeting will be taken over by Agent Roy. I have to leave urgently. Agent Roy, continue with the next issue." – grabbing her file and walking briskly towards the doors of the hall – "Agent Rao, come with me, please! Quickly!" said the Chair while still walking.

The LSS Director immediately got up with her files and went following behind. They go out the doors into the corridor towards the lift and enter it. They get off at the 35th floor, out of 40, and walk across the corridor into the cabin of the Chair. The LSS Director closed the door and the Chair was still standing while massaging her forehead with irritation.

"Prakash escaped just a while ago. The phone call was from one of the agents on his tail right now!" she said.

What the…

The Director did not reply.

"Well? What do you have to say?" she asked.

"What can you expect me to say?" she asked back.

"You know him better than anybody! Now give a solution! Why else do you think I gave a good word for you to become the LSS Director?" she said.

"And I can't thank you enough, Manisha! Anyway, we'll have to get him since obviously killing him is not the solution yet." She replied.

"You said you had a solution to find his old company. Care to tell?" she asked.

The Director brooded a little while turning the ring on her finger.

"Okay, first, his company is still there. Second, he has less manpower with him. So, he and his associates will be going in person to handle their business. We need to apprehend one member making a deal. And once we do then we'll get to know about everything." She replied.

"With Intel, we can help but who do you plan on sending for the arrest and recovery?" she asked.

"My top 50 ranked agents." She said.

"That cannot be authorized. They are minors. Don't be crazy!" She said.

"They are very good. They won't let you down." Said the Director, requesting her.

"Yes, that robbery attempt on your LOCKER…but it's dangerous. They are too young. They are unauthorised." She said.

"In LSS guidelines, they can do something this dangerous. Come on, they haven't received a mission! In 10 years!" said the Director.

"Hmm…I guess I can allow that seeing that this comes under their jurisdiction. But a few agents under me will be in charge. They must obey. So, an interpreter of the squad is needed." She said.

"I already know whom to choose. She's very good." Said the Director.

"Who is she?" she asked.

"Agent Simran Khanna." She replied.

"One of the highest scorers…Khanna? Agent Khanna's daughter?" she asked.

"Relations don't matter. Give me permission for the investigation, ma'am. I won't let you down." She said.

"That's not the issue. I don't want anyone getting to know about this or else you might get fired. Are you ready for that?" she asked.

"Yes, ma'am." She said.

"Fine, then. I'll have an agent inform you if we get any intel on a deal." She said.

She nodded and they shook hands.

After a couple of days, Simran landed in New Delhi by a flight. After walking out of the airport, she found a taxi, asked a place to go and got in after the driver nodded yes. The taxi drove for a while and reached a locality giving a familiar vibe to her. She stopped the taxi in front of a street.

"Just wait a minute." She instructed the driver and got down. She was wearing a black hoodie and she walked forward to the third two-floored cream coloured house on the right of the street. She stopped and walked over to a window. It had a paint stain on it.

Still didn't get it off, huh dad? Mom said it was permanent when we got the house painted.

She peered through the window while hiding behind the ledge and saw her living room and kitchen, one after the other. A man was sitting on a chair reading a book.

Dad…

Just then, a young man of almost 25 appeared from the kitchen with two mugs of either coffee or soup and handed one mug over to the man reading while sitting down on a chair near him. He took his carefully with a small smile.

He came back! Shit! I should just meet the director and get out of Delhi!

Simran right then went back to her taxi as soon as she got a good look at the young man's face. She got in the taxi and they left.

Inside the house, the two men sat down with their coffee mugs and began to watch TV. After some time, Simran's father placed his cup on a table, opened his laptop and started typing while looking intently at the screen.

"I heard a car outside." Said the young man, trying to look out the window from a distance.

"It might be nothing. You get disturbed easily." He replied.

"What if it's- "he started.

"You think Simran will come home so easily? After what you did?" he interrupted him.

"It's not a- "he again started.

"Of course, it is a big deal! I really suggest therapy for you." He said, without looking at him.

The young man silently folded his hands in a fit.

"What happened? I'm not saying unreasonable things, *beta*." Said her father.

Saying that last word was always a habit of his to all those younger than him. It was shown as a comfort word to those close to him, especially to the shooting teacher of Simran.

"I don't need therapy. I can handle my life well." he replied.

"I can see that." Said her father sarcastically with a bit of a chuckle.

The driver dropped Simran off with her bag at a normal hotel almost at another side of the city and she checked into a room after paying the taxi driver. She unlocked her room, closed the door and relaxed for an hour till she heard a soft knock on the door. She got up and went to the door. She peeked outside through the peephole and sighed in relief. She opened it and it was the LSS Director.

"Good you called me here…less attention." She said, coming inside and shutting the door after her.

"I have a feeling that this discussion is unofficial, ma'am." Said Simran.

"I'll just get to the point because I've got a lot of work. Okay?" said the Director, sitting down on a chair.

Simran nods slightly and sits down on another chair.

"Here, take this and remember it…" – handing over a slip of paper – "I want you to keep checking this website while you are at school. Make sure your device is untraceable.

Check every day. Don't worry if nothing happens at first. This website is currently inactive. You will only find the homepage accessible now. When the website becomes active, other pages on it will become updated. Understood?" she instructed.

"Okay. Why am I being given this?" She asked.

"I can't trust cybercrimes for Prakash related affairs. If you've seen the news, then you know that he and Brad escaped. So just do it." she said.

That quickly?! My god…

Simran took the slip, gave it a quick glance, folded it and stuffed it in her pocket.

"What sort of information do you want me to find out?" asked Simran.

"Anything if you can hack in. So far, just check when it gets active." She replied.

"That's it?" asked Simran.

"Pretty much…after that you will be going on your first top 50 mission. Be prepared for it. You'll be an interpreter/advisor." Said the Director.

"Yes, ma'am." Said Simran.

They get up and go towards the door when the Director stops and turns around towards her.

"Is there any problem going on between you and your father? I'm asking as a family friend here." Said the Director.

"No, it's nothing to worry about." Replied Simran.

"All right, then. I'll be going now. You get back to school quickly and start." She said.

"Yes, ma'am." Said Simran.

The Director opened the door and left the room. A while later, Simran grabbed her backpack and left soon after to the airport by catching another taxi. She reached and left by a flight to Guwahati.

Near the India-Bhutan border was the Rohtang Residential School. For now, it was empty due to the term ending vacations with only a few agents on patrol. The one sacrifice for the LSS agents was to patrol even more during holidays. They may leave for a day or two if there is an emergency but most of them had to stay at school. Arjun and Gaurav were walking in the empty corridors alone together. While they walked,

"This is awkward…" said Arjun. "I mean, this situation…"

"Your snooping made it more awkward than ever." said Gaurav, not caring.

As usual, Arjun hates Simran but Gaurav now became her friend which makes them not get along. Now that Nikhil partnered them up for the holidays, they have no choice but to wait until Simran gets back. While the vacations went on, many agents left home. Only a few patrolled the campus.

Nikhil and Natasha, instead of patrolling, were mostly in the Principal's cabin, discussing more security measures to be taken by them. Nikhil never trusted Arjun in the first place and ever since he became in charge of their team, he's been extra careful. Also, after the robbery attempt, he's prohibited many things for the agents. And the top 400 agents must obey since he is top 50. Indira went home for a while and she has no idea on what he's doing.

Radhika spent most of her time outside the school campus from the early morning till the afternoon. She visits the nearest army base sometimes but mostly she became acquainted with the LSS Director's private defence sector officers. She's allowed by the Principal to go so yes; Nikhil can't say anything. Per the Principal's recent message to them, a few officers are to patrol the nearby town every now and then. Radhika practices some combat and shooting at the defence sector with the officers and learnt quite a lot from them.

I'll have to be ready for the coming top 50 mission Simran told me about...she might be in charge for it huh...

She thought while shooting targets with other officers.

Raghav and Priya began working out in the school gym. Priya became frightened of Simran when the fight during the robbery attempt was going on. She admired her to an extent later, mostly because Simran was one of the only people who retort back at Nikhil, Aakash and Arjun. Raghav, on the other hand, never stopped thinking about Radhika and how strong she is and he started hating Gaurav. Also, he merely passed the mark of getting into the top 50 that he was determined to prove his worth.

"Aren't you getting tired, Raghav?" asked Priya.

"No way. But you seem tired." He said, sweating profusely.

"No, I am not. Don't get your hopes up about" – seeing him suddenly glancing at Radhika passing by – "…Radhika. Can't you forget about your dating needs for just these couple months?" She said, annoyed.

"It's my habit! Deal with it! She'll come over…one day." He said.

"Don't kid yourself!" she said.

Finally, Arjun stayed in the surveillance room for most of the time while Gaurav hung around with Radhika at school. When she left, he would come to the surveillance.

Coming back, the awkward situation that occurred between Arjun and Gaurav was on that same day when Simran wasn't there. Gaurav had gone to the girls' hostel side and directly went up to the fifth floor to check Radhika's room. It was locked from the outside.

She must've left to the base again…what does she even do there?

He sighed, turned around and was just about to go when he suddenly heard something crash down with a thump in the room adjacent to Radhika's.

What was that?

He turned back around and rushed over to the room door and opened it wide to see a closet shaken and a box with a lock on the floor! He also saw Arjun sitting down and leaning against a wall while rubbing his forehead.

"What the hell are you doing?!" exclaimed Gaurav.

"None of your business! Get lost!" said Arjun.

"It's none of your business to be here!" said Gaurav, folding his hands.

"Get out!" he said.

"Do you even think you'll be able to open any of them?" asked Gaurav.

"Why? It can't be that hard!" he said.

"It's Simran we're talking about." He said.

Gaurav went and tilted the box upwards which had a lock in the middle.

I guess a locksmith is enough to see this…seriously, a lock? That's it?

He felt the lock and lifted it to see no keyhole at the bottom. Instead, there was a groove in it with a small, black-papered screen embedded. It was a fingerprint scanner. Simran's father had given it to her but she and Radhika modified it.

Damn…now I feel more curious…what is wrong with me? No, I'm not going to snoop through her stuff!

He put the box back up on the closet and pushed it towards the wall for its stability.

"Come on! It's not possible to see what's inside. Before Radhika comes, let's go! Get up!" said Gaurav, tugging Arjun's arm and getting him up on his feet.

"Come on, it's a lock. We need a key, right?" said Arjun.

"The key is Simran's fingerprint. So just leave it." Said Gaurav and dragged him away out of the room.

Back to their conversation after this happened, while they walked in the corridor,

"This is awkward…" said Arjun. "I mean, this situation…"

"Your snooping made it more awkward than ever." Said Gaurav, not caring.

Arjun stopped and looked directly at him.

"I mean…okay! I wanted to see too but, uh…no." said Gaurav, looking away from him.

"Why not?" he asked.

"Because, she's my friend now!" he replied.

"How can you be friends with a girl like her? She's such a know it all! So annoying!" said Arjun, walking forward.

How can you not?

Gaurav goes ahead and stops him.

"You're lying." He said, sternly looking at him.

"I don't have to say anything to you!" said Arjun.

"I seriously wonder how can anyone be friends with you. You never listen to what others have to say at all!" said Gaurav.

"Oh, come on!" he said.

"What 'Oh, come on'? That's why everybody hates you, man!" said Gaurav.

"Which I'm totally fine with!" he said.

"You're lying!" he said again.

He was silent.

"Well, now you're listening. Good. But I'm done talking to you. You think you have good friends now, but you see. You screw up again, then even Nikhil will leave you!" said Gaurav and left walking ahead.

"Get over it! It was one time!" he said.

"I did! Nikhil will never because he is too damn selfish!" –
turning around – "Did you ever think that maybe those
friends of yours aren't really friends?" asked Gaurav.

"Why do you say that?" asked Arjun.

"Because they are ruining the team! Your friend Raghav is
annoying me like hell! Nikhil just behaves like a boss as if
he's so great and Natasha is not anything but she dictates us!
My life is already screwed up enough!" said Gaurav and left.

Chapter Two – Back to school, back to duty.

The vacations came to an end. Everyone from school was at the train station to receive their friends. School bus and van drivers were ready in the parking lot as well and the rest of the agents were also back.

Indira arrived at Platform 3 and got off the train with her back pack. She turned left towards the bridge and stopped midway. Someone had come to receive her and it was surprising to Indira.

"Good that you're back!" said Priya, standing in front of her
with a jacket on.

What's up with her suddenly?

"Nobody was supposed to receive me. What's going on?"
asked Indira, puzzled.

"I came to kill you because of you just leaving! How could
you just leave us alone like this?! Where the hell did you go?!
Nikhil was…" Priya started scolding as her face darkened
with anger.

Oh my god! And I thought there was something wrong with her!

"Priya! Hey!" called out a voice from behind Indira.

It was Ankita with her bag.

"Oh! Hey! I was waiting for you! Come on!" said Priya.

She had suddenly stopped ranting to Indira and went up
the bridge with Ankita as if nothing happened. Indira stood
there and sighed.

Yup, that was weird!

She started walking up the bridge.

I really shouldn't have come back now. I still had work to do at home but these rules…

She reached the top to see Simran and Radhika waiting and talking.

"Hey, Indu! Want me to carry the bag for you?" asked Radhika.

"Yeah, if you don't mind." Said Indira and gave her bag to Radhika.

"So, you went home again?" asked Simran.

"I go all the time but I don't miss much duty. I still don't know how I was made an in-charge." Said Indira.

"Is Aakash the reason to always go home?" asked Radhika.

"Yeah, pretty much. He's bothersome." She replied.

"I've heard that Nikhil has been tormenting everybody." Said Simran.

"Yeah, Priya told me everything. Maybe I should get Shreya to kick some sense into him." said Indira.

"No, he can get her in trouble. She's not top 50." Said Radhika.

"Then what should I do?" asked Indira.

"Take charge yourself." Said Simran.

"Hmm..." said Indira.

They walked out and into one of the school cars.

"Settled down?" asked Simran, after the three of them sat inside.

"Yeah, all good." Said Radhika.

"Okay, let's go!" said Simran to the driver.

He gave a friendly nod and started the car. They left the station.

Meanwhile, at school, Neerav was with Shreya and Gaurav in the canteen. He was a bit worried and anxious. They were all waiting near a queue near the counter as the food was delayed. They haven't joined the line yet. Shreya was a bit impatient whereas Gaurav was deep into a novel.

"Hey, what's wrong? You've been like this since morning!" said Shreya, noticing.

"Yeah, what's up with you?" asked Gaurav, while still looking into his kindle.

"I haven't heard anything from Rishi. No phone call, no text message, nothing. I'm just hoping he comes back soon. I hope he gets back." Said Neerav, getting nervous as the students started coming for dinner.

"He'll be here. He needs some time." Said Shreya, putting her hand on his shoulder giving a slight squeeze.

"Shouldn't it be good if he's home?" asked Gaurav, looking up at them.

"No, I want to keep an eye on him here and he can't violate the rules of staying away from duty. If he's here, then he will stay out of trouble." Said Neerav.

"It's only been a week. He'll be back. Let's eat now." Said Gaurav, noticing the counter finally functional.

"Just a bit longer. Please." Said Neerav.

Just then, Gaurav looked up to see Indira, Simran and Radhika come with their plates. They come to their table and sit down. Radhika held out her hand in front of Gaurav.

"What?" he asked.

"Give the tablet to me. Then get your food." Said Radhika.

"But a good part is coming." He said.

"Well, it's not going anywhere." Said Simran.

He switches it off and gives it to her. She takes it and he gets up and goes to get his food. Shreya and Neerav go and get their dinner as well. They start talking and eating. Simran, as usual, eats a lot so she was still eating at the table alone even when everybody left. Arjun had arrived, quickly grabbed a plate and sat down in front of Simran.

"There are empty chairs everywhere. Why don't- "started Simran.

"Most people would say 'Hi' or 'Hey'!" said Arjun.

"They say it to a friend. Not people like you." She said.

"Whatever, we're partners." said Arjun.

"Only for the few hours we have to spend at duty. I can't handle you more than that." Said Simran.

"Whatever. I'm going to be hanging around with you for quite a bit off-duty as well, whether you like it or not, Miss know it all!" said Arjun.

"Huh, with me? Why?" she asked, bewildered.

"You know why." He said.

"Oh, because someone needs to catch you when you faint again- "started Simran.

"Shh!" Arjun interrupted.

They looked at a side to see the group of Nikhil, Natasha, Siddharth, Aanya, Aneesh and Ankita going then Aakash, each giving a look at them and going.

"Oh…sorry…" she said.

She had finished her food and looked around to see nobody else except a few staff cleaning the tables. One of them looked at her, smiled and motioned her to continue as they had no hurry. Arjun noticed that while still eating.

"Well, well, well! You have friends everywhere, huh." He said.

"They are way better than your gang will ever be." she said.

"They're not that bad." he said.

"Yeah, I'm still trying to convince myself about it. They never care about the team." She said.

"They do. They just…won't show it." he said.

"They think their way of doing things is the best way." She said.

"I can say the same to you." He said.

"Just eat quickly, I want to go back." She said, impatiently.

They kept their plates and left the canteen. While they walked,

"I'm just mentioning this now; we might get a mission soon." Said Simran.

"Okay…and I'm guessing you might be the head." He said.

"No, we have many agents above us. I'm just an interpreter." she said.

"But we have to listen to you." He said.

"So, you got a problem with that, huh." She said.

He did not answer and just gave a look.

"Do you?" she asked, puzzled.

"The walls have ears." He said.

They reached the hostels common ground floor and left to their individual dorms. Arjun hid upstairs and checked to see Simran going up. As soon as she did, he came back down and was about to leave the hostels.

"Where are you going?" Nikhil asked, just when Arjun turned his back.

Arjun turned around slowly.

"Oh, you. I thought Simran." He sighed with relief.

"You two had dinner together all this time. Should I be concerned?" he asked.

"Hey, you told me to be nice to her." He said.

"Just for the sake of duty. But anyway, you going into town? Now?" asked Nikhil, folding his hands.

"Yeah, just for a bit. Small deal. Only one guy wants one item." He said.

"You mean, the most expensive one you have." Said Nikhil, grimly.

"Come on, man. I am very careful with these things." Said Arjun.

Yeah, but not careful enough about the LOCKER…I swear, your deals are more frequent this time, Arjun. Why can't you just let me go? Ever since the vacations started, you are always going without my notice.

"Lights out by 10:30 pm. If you get back late, call me." Said Nikhil and left upstairs.

Arjun sneaked out of the hostel gate in his hoodie. Just then, Gaurav noticed someone going outside the hostel gate, getting on a bike and riding away. His face was too far to be seen.

Who's going out so late after hours? Is it Nikhil? Maybe Ajay… must be Ajay.

The next day was a Sunday and early in the morning Simran went to the hidden meeting room with Radhika and silently turned on her laptop as Radhika sat next to her after locking the door. Simran opened the website to check.

The homepage opened. Simran clicked on another links but nothing happened.

"Is this supposed to happen?" asked Radhika.

"It's not activated yet." Said Simran.

She frowned and closed the laptop. They left back to their hostel rooms, changed and went down to the parking. They grab a bike and go outside the school. They keep driving on the highway and reach the nearby town. They stop at the local police station. Radhika gets down and goes inside. A few constables sitting there waved and greeted her. She gave a look to them and one of them reached in his pocket and gave a crumpled paper in her hand. She nodded and left. She got on the bike and left with Simran.

They get back on the highway and reach the defence sector. They were stopped at the gate. Radhika showed her badge. The guard saw it and motioned to the other officers allowing them to pass.

After a couple of days passed with Simran and Radhika still not finding anything else on the website still. In the lunch break, the occasional meeting for the partner shuffling was there in the meeting room.

"So let's- "Nikhil started.

"All right, I've pre-planned. At the north gate, it's Aakash and Priya. South gate has Gaurav and Radhika. Raghav and Aanya at the west gate. Siddharth and Shreya at the South gate. I and Aneesh, hostels. School main building, Ankita and Neerav. Nikhil and Natasha in the ground. Got it?" said Indira, reading out the list in her notepad.

"Yes!" everybody beamed happily.

"Hey! Weren't you supposed to discuss with me first?!" exclaimed Nikhil.

"You got your fun when I wasn't there, Nikhil." said Indira.

"Anything else?" asked Aakash.

"No!" said Indira, with a stern look and left to the Principal's cabin.

After spending an hour there, she left to the hostels and packed her bag. Then she left in a school car to the station.

"She left again, huh." Said Simran.

"Yeah…" said Radhika.

They both were with Gaurav in the basketball court shooting while everybody else were outside the campus.

"Does she have to be here?" asked Gaurav.

"Not yet…" said Simran.

Gaurav was still puzzled.

"I mean; we're still checking but nothing's happening." She said and shot a ball in the hoop.

"That's not good, then. But we have other things to worry about." Said Gaurav.

"Like what?" asked Radhika.

"One thing is that Rishi is missing. And Siddharth's girlfriend is as well, although that doesn't matter now." He said, while dribbling.

"Rishi still didn't come?" Radhika was surprised.

"Yeah, I don't know what's going on with him. He should be here or else he's suspended from duty. And maybe expelled from school. Plus, we've got exams in a few months and teachers are hell bent on finishing portion by December." He said.

"He shouldn't be gone for that long. I'm getting a little worried. Should we track him?" asked Radhika.

"It's okay, I can understand how he's feeling. Let him be for now. He's still hurt." Said Simran.

"But still- "Radhika started.

"It's none of your business. Just keep your distance from it." Said Nikhil, coming with Natasha, Raghav and Aakash.

The three of them turned around to see the entire gang of Nikhil, Natasha, Aakash and Raghav approaching them.

"What do you want, Nikhil?" asked Simran, annoyed.

"I just overheard what you guys were talking about so we decided to join you." Said Aakash.

"So, others answer for you, Agent Patel?" taunted Gaurav.

"You shouldn't be making hasty decisions regarding our friend." Said Natasha.

"Rishi is a teammate and we all get to care about him." Said Radhika.

"Come on, babes! Just leave the matter. We'll handle it." Said Raghav.

"You have a death wish, idiot?!" growled Radhika in her moderate anger.

Annoying idiot! How dare he call me that again?!

"How about you get lost from here?! You're too dumb to be talking to us anyway!" said Gaurav, irritated.

"Make me!" he said.

Gaurav was about to take a step forward when Radhika grabbed his hand and pulled him back.

"Avoid!" she whispered.

Simran walked forward and stopped a foot away from Nikhil with her hands folded.

"You think you're so great just waltzing in the LSS, impressing everybody you can, huh!" said Nikhil.

"Well, I don't have to try, unlike you." – stepping forward and looking fiercely into his eyes – "I can tell that you're so jealous." Said Simran.

"You don't know me or what I'm capable of. Don't mess with me or my squad." He said.

"Or what? You'll complain? Get me fired?" said Simran, taunting him.

"Stay off Rishi's case or else…" he threatened.

"Stay off ours first!" – catching Nikhil's punch in her hand firmly –"Never think you are better than me. Never think you can find anything about me to use against me. Never think you can dictate me whatever or else I won't save your useless ass again." Replied Simran, calmly.

"So just leave before I- "Radhika started threatening.

"Before you what? You think you can just beat any of us in anything?!" said Natasha. "You piece of-"

"Natasha! Avoid!" said Arjun, putting one hand on her shoulder and the other on Nikhil.

"No way!" said Raghav.

Just then the bell rang.

"Let's go, guys. Leave them be. We've got stuff to do." Said Arjun, while looking at Simran.

Aakash gave one look and left dragging Raghav with him. Nikhil and Natasha left after a glare. Arjun left after them with his hands in the front pockets of his hoodie.

At duty time later, in the Surveillance room,

"You're welcome." Said Arjun, standing next to Simran in front of the cameras.

"What's gotten into you? You just broke up a fight when you initiate it." She said.

"Be thankful I did." He replied.

A pause occurred.

What's up with him? I can't fight with her so he should?

"So, what was the deal anyway? Nikhil does get pissed off easily." Asked Arjun.

"Well…gist is that he doesn't want us to track down Rishi saying that it's none of our business." Said Simran.

"He needs time…it's only been a month since Aparna died." Said Arjun.

"You were also her friend once, right?" asked Simran.

"I don't know about that. I talked to her a few times. But yeah, my mind is not in the right space now." He replied.

"What do you mean?" she asked.

"I'm not liking what's going on now. I don't feel good about any of this. Aparna's killer is still out there, so being Prakash. And you said that Brad is with him, everybody's out there. They are free. We may get killed anytime. I'm surprised they haven't come yet." He said.

"So, you're worried about something, huh. I never expected that from you." She said.

"I'm serious." he said.

"Well, that means they have other business to take care of because more than half of their men have either been bought or killed. They have to regroup." She said.

"How long do you think that will take?" he asked.

She didn't answer.

"Hey, listen…" he said, putting his hand on her shoulder and she turned towards him.

"I don't know if my health is getting better or worse but I'm freaked out a bit. Aren't you?" he asked.

"Must really be serious if you're getting scared." she said, taunting him.

"I really want to punch your face in." He said.

"I don't require a reason for doing that to you." She said.

They glared at each other with a pause.

"How did you shoot the guy to save me? You shot him, right?" he asked, still glaring at her.

"I'm not saying anything. Just focus." She said, turning back to the cameras.

Chapter Three – New mission!

After a couple of days, Simran and Radhika again snuck into the meeting room and went to the website. While it was loading,

"We've been at this for a week! How much longer?" asked Radhika, annoyed.

"I'm fed up too. But we have to keep checking." Said Simran. The website's homepage opened showing the same format intact. But on one of the hyperlinks there was a star marked.

That wasn't there before…

Simran clicked on the link and it started loading. It took quite some time.

Come on, please load…

A new page opened! It loaded a few things.

"Yes! Yes! Yes! The site's active! Finally!" said Radhika, happily.

"Go turn on the link! The Director has to know and we have to discuss!" said Simran.

Radhika turns on the webcam of a computer in the meeting room and accessed the link in it. It loaded. After a few minutes, it turned on. The Director's face was seen.

"Agents Khanna and Chopra…are you alone?" asked the Director.

"Yes, ma'am!" said Radhika.

"All right, update me!" said the Director.

"The website came back online. The links can be opened now but we need an account. Only those registered can access the rest of it." Said Simran.

"Hmm…" she thought, while turning the ring on her finger.

They all did for a minute or two.

"Okay, that'll be all, girls." Said the Director.

"Are you sure, ma'am?" asked Simran.

"I can handle this! Leave it to me!" said the Director.

"But how will you access it? Hacking into it is still a bit difficult, even for us." asked Radhika.

"There is a high chance that Prakash accessed a couple deals from this computer." said the Director.

Both agents were puzzled.

"Just a minute!" she said and began typing something on the keyboard.

"Ah! I'm sure it was here! I'm getting your father, Simran. He can get it." Said the Director.

"That's lucky." Said Simran.

"All right. I've got work to do. You will get details on your mission very shortly. Okay?" said the Director.

"Okay." They said.

The screen turned black. The Director had disconnected.

"Dad will get something, I'm sure!" said Simran.

"Yeah. Speaking of him, did you guys talk?" Said Radhika.

"Nope. It's not safe to." Said Simran.

"It's been a few months, Simran. You guys should talk it out. All three of you." She said.

"We'll see about that later, okay?" she said.

Radhika was silent. She started thinking for a while.

"What happened?" asked Simran.

"How will we work with the top 50? We'll keep fighting, Simran. It'll be hard." Said Radhika.

"These criminals are dangerous and anyway, we all want to get something out of this. So we will find a way." Said Simran.

"As long as we listen to the agents in charge, we'll be fine. Right?" Said Radhika.

Right...I guess...

Simran thought.

The next day, during the break time, Simran calls up Indira.

"Yeah, Simran!" she answered.

"Is everything fine at home?" asked Simran.

"Uh, yeah! Just a couple more days. Why?" she asked.

"In two days, you have to get back. We'll have a meeting regarding our top 50 mission, okay?" said Simran.

"Two days?! Oh!" she said, shocked.

"What? Don't decline! You got no choice!" said Simran.

"I know, I know! I got it! When's the meeting? What time?" she asked.

"Sometime during break. Be there." Said Simran.

"I got it. I'll be there." Said Indira. "Bye!"

The phone call was cut.

I wonder what's going on at her house…

Radhika came over and sat down next to Simran in the study hall.

"What did she say?" she asked.

"She said that she'll be there. I really wonder what's so important that she's home now!" said Simran.

"Let's see, we'll ask her." Said Radhika.

A couple of days later, on one morning at break time, in the meeting room, all top 50 qualified agents just entered with the Principal. She closed the door after everybody settled down.

"All right! Everyone here?" asked Nikhil.

"Yeah!" said Raghav.

"Wait! Indu's not!" said Radhika.

"Where is she?" asked Aakash.

"I'm not sure. She said that her train would reach in the morning." Said Nikhil.

"She'll be here any- "started Simran when Indira had suddenly come in with her bag pack and closed the door.

She directly arrived from the station. She was wearing a light purple sweater having a turtle neck and full sleeved and wearing a pair of tight black jeans with sneakers. That wasn't the reason why everybody was wide eyed. What did was that her hair was open and only above her shoulder!

"Glad you could make it, Indu. Have a seat!" said Nikhil, speaking first.

"Yeah, thanks." She said and sat down next to Simran near the door.

"What's with the new hair?" Simran whispered.

"I'll tell you later…" Indira whispered back.

"All right! Our mission requires two days, starting tomorrow. An early morning flight, some planning to do, next day evening is the job and another early morning flight, just in time for school. No absence at all." Said Nikhil.

"What a pain! No sleep?" asked Arjun.

"No choice. Exams are from December second week and your syllabus is not complete yet. Keep continuing, I've got work to do." Said the Principal and left the room, closing the door after her.

"Well, you know our lazy teachers. We even have most of our competitions cancelled this year. Ma'am will announce that." Said Nikhil.

"Damn…" Gaurav muttered.

"More than that, we need to focus on our mission here. It cannot go wrong or else we're done for. It's top class. I've heard that RA&W had a problem doing it. We'll have to listen to many top agents over there." Said Indira.

Everybody became silent. Indira continued.

"Our target is" – slamming down a photograph on the table of a young Chinese woman – "Lu. An associate of Prakash. She is on route to Chennai for a contract shipping business deal for their company with a buyer. Then she'll leave on a flight to New Zealand." She explained.

"What's the shipment?" asked Natasha.

"Two large wooden crates filled with hay concealing snipers made from the best country: Russia. It may also have AK-47s depending on the size." Said Indira.

"So, what's our mission exactly?" asked Gaurav.

"Arrest Lu and acquire the shipment then hand it over to the officials of the IB in Chennai. We get some answers from her and the shipment for clues." Said Indira.

"Clear?" asked Nikhil.

"Yes!" they said.

"All right, let's go!" said Nikhil.

"Woah! Wait a minute!" said Radhika.

Everyone who had stood sat back down.

"Are you sure you said everything?" asked Radhika.

"Yeah!" said Nikhil.

"Really? Is there anything else you'd like us to know or shall we ask Princi?" asked Radhika.

How does she know? How can she tell?

Nikhil didn't say a word.

"Care to enlighten us, then?" asked Natasha.

"Since this mission is top class, the Director must have chosen a mission interpreter amongst us. And you didn't mention it because it's not you! Am I right?" said Radhika.

Nikhil remained silent.

"Who's the in charge?" asked Aakash.

"Simran…" Nikhil said in a low voice filled with temper.

Everybody was wide eyed at that. Simran said nothing.

"That's not fair!" shouted out Aakash.

"It is, actually!" said Indira. "I'm fine with her!"

"I'm not! I won't follow orders from a girl like her!" said Raghav.

"That's surprising from you, Raghav! I'd expect to hear that from Arjun!" said Natasha, which then made everybody turn to Arjun.

"What?" he asked.

"Well, are you fine with Simran as the interpreter?" asked Nikhil.

"Uh…" Arjun hesitated.

"Such a coward…" murmured Gaurav.

Simran turned to see Arjun as well.

"I'm fine with her!" he said, looking at her.

"Really?" asked Radhika.

"What the…" Raghav was astounded.

"Well, seeing that most of us are comfortable with this, there's no need to object now!" said Gaurav.

"Yeah. So, pack up and we'll leave in a cab I booked at 4 in the morning tomorrow. Meeting's adjourned." Said Indira and left.

Everybody left the meeting room except Arjun and Simran. Arjun closed the door and locked it after stopping her from leaving the room.

"What's going on?" asked Simran.

He came up to her and stopped a foot away with a stern look on his face.

"I have two conditions if you want me to be willing to work with you." Said Arjun.

No wonder he was okay with me being in charge. Great, what conditions will he put?

"Okay. Tell me." She said.

"First condition! Keep me with you all the time over there." He said.

"Huh? Why?"

"You know why. I told you before!"

"All the time?! I can't do that! I can't handle you for more than four hours!"

"You don't have a choice."

"Oh really! How come?"

"You don't want to jeopardize the mission, do you?"

"Are you kidding me?"

"Does it look like I'm kidding?"

"So, in a way, me not keeping an eye on you will jeopardize the mission? Come on! Don't act so weak!"

"I'm not weak! This rarely happens and I'm really having a problem-"

"You can't be serious. Suddenly, have you stopped believing yourself or something?"

"Accept it like that."

"So out of the blue, you'll faint? And I have to take care of you?!"

"Oh yes."

"You trust that I'll do this?"

"No, but it's your responsibility if you want to make sure we don't screw up the mission."

"I'll hate you even more for this, you piece of-"

"Same here!"

They said nothing.

"But fine! I'll do it because now, I'm actually getting worried about you too! What's the next condition?" she said.

"How did you save me that day?"

"I'll tell you later."

"No, now!"

"Not now. Please."

"Why not? I deserve to know!"

"Knowing nothing about me is for the best. At least for now."

"Are you telling me that I can't know anything about you when you know almost everything about me? Huh?"

"I never asked you to tell me!" she shouted, while thumping his head once.

He was about to raise his hand but instead he became silent.

"Right now, we need to focus on the mission." She said and opened the door to go.

"So, my first condition?" asked Arjun, massaging his head.

"Yeah, I'll be with you. Always." She said, angrily and left while closing it.

He sighed in annoyance. Just then she opened the door and bent inside.

"Just saying, you might want to clean your shirt properly this time because Riya's foundation is stuck on the back." She said.

"What?" – pulling his shirt while looking back to see some powdery substance – "How did you-" he started.

"Her room is next to mine and whenever she feels like picking a fight, I can smell the foundation metres away. It smells gross." She said and left.

"It's not what you think!" he called out but she was gone.

Shit...wait! She's checking me out a lot nowadays...not that I'm complaining...whatever. This stupid Riya should stop touching me or else...

Chapter Four – Major Pal.

The next morning, the agents at school were about to see off the top 50. Before getting into the taxi booked, Gaurav pulled Siddharth to a corner.

"Look, I know you don't like talking about her nowadays, but do you think she left the school only because of your break up?" asked Gaurav, seriously.

"Dude, you worry too much! She left because of me and that one teacher humiliating her. It's normal." Siddharth replied.

"Sorry, I'm just getting suspicious about everybody leaving and not coming back. But on another note, Rishi is still missing. The police have a lot of missing people to find. The nearby town is not well known to us and- "he started.

"What do you want me to do?" he asked.

"Check the nearby town for him. His phone was traced there. A faint signal but it was there. Don't be sarcastic and helpless like this." Said Gaurav.

"Hey, I'm under you! Your top 50. I'm ready to listen to you, Radhika and Simran. Nobody else. Just tell me what to do." Said Siddharth.

"Really? You'll listen to me? No offense, but I never liked any of you. I don't know you either but still…" he said.

"Trust me on this. Just tell me what to do!" he said.

"I want you to request Princi to assign two agents to keep checking out the nearby town. Yes, I know they may not get enough sleep but it's important." Said Gaurav.

"You got it. Now go for your mission." Said Siddharth.

"Thanks, man!" said Gaurav and left.

They bid adieu to the top 50 and the cab left.

The top 50 landed in the Meenambakkam International airport at 8:00 in the morning. They came out the airport and went into a big taxi. They drove for around half an hour and reached a small alley where they got down with their bags. They started walking inside.

"Where the hell are we going, Simran?" asked Raghav.

"Oh! Here we are!" she said as they reached a dead end.

They stopped in front of a warehouse. It was old and battered. The paint was fresh on some parts. Simran unlocked a door to the left side and they all entered. It was dark inside.

"Ow!" said Radhika, suddenly.

Someone fell while bumping into her. Arjun found the lights and turned them on. They all saw Radhika on the ground with Raghav on top of her.

"Get off- "started Radhika.

"Get off her!" said Gaurav, angrily and pulled Raghav off. Radhika got up and dusted herself.

The warehouse consisted of a huge hall with one bathroom, two rooms and one small room. A door to one room had opened and three to four people, two men and two women came out with a few police and stood in front of them. One well built, tall and dark man with a beard took a step forward.

"Attention!" he said.

Everybody put their bags down and stood erect in a line.

"I am Major Pal, in charge of this mission. With me are these people whose names you can ask later. You will address me by Major Pal. Nothing more, nothing less. Understood?" he instructed.

"Yes, sir!" they replied in unison.

"My decisions are final in this particular mission. But we respect your jurisdiction in this case. Clear?" he said.

"Yes, sir!" they replied.

"Well, keep your bags and come outside. We'll plan! Quickly!" he ordered.

Everybody went into the two large rooms and kept their bags. Radhika kept Simran's bag while Simran was called by Major Pal and she pulled a huge table to the middle, dusted it and pulled out a map on her tablet and kept it on the table. He then took out a sheet of paper and a marker and started making points and dots on it. She then pushed a button on her tablet and held it above the paper.

"Sorry, the operation is too covert for me to even get proper blueprints." Said Major Pal.

"It's all right, sir." She said.

After an hour, everyone arrived and stood around Simran, looking at the schematic map that projected off the tablet. They all were shocked.

"Everything done?" asked Major Pal.

"Yes, sir." She said.

"All right, before we go out to scour the area of our operation, I'll just state a few rules." Said Major Pal.

Everyone listened intently and basic rules were explained while did not please half of the members since it concerned Simran being in charge with interpreting them.

"Okay, gather around. This map has the area where she most likely will be. There is a hotel on one side and just half a kilometre away is a dockyard. With a little Intel from the cops here, her shipment is here." – pointing at the hotel – "And at the docks the deal will take place tomorrow at 10:30

pm sharp. But before that, she's attending a banquet at the hotel. I don't know why but it's like that." Major Pal explained.

"So we'll split up outside in pairs with an in-charge agent, me being alone with Major Pal. Each pair should have one camera with them. We've got three hours in the area. Spend it wisely. First up, Natasha and Radhika, you both will check out the docks. Aakash and Indira, check out the sewage drains. Nikhil and Raghav, you two go on the terraces of the buildings and take pictures, also the corridors of the hotel, wherever a camera is there. Lastly, Arjun and Gaurav, you both check out the cameras of the hotels, disguised. The hotel must be having a problem with the CCTV cameras. I will meet the hotel security and an officer and talk about the schedule of tomorrow. Got it?" said Simran, interpreting.

"Got it!" everybody said.

"Let's go! After your done, get back to the warehouse straightaway. Understood?" said Major Pal.

"Got it!" they said.

The top 50 left the warehouse, split up and began their investigation with their respective agents.

Meanwhile, at school, in the Principal's cabin,

"But ma'am, it's required. You know how much it's getting dangerous!" said Siddharth.

"Agent Bhattacharya, you are to protect the school and the school only. It is not required for patrolling the nearby town. The nearest army base and the police are more than enough. I've even sent orders to them." Said the Principal.

"I'm only asking a small search for any missing person clues!" he said.

"Are you undermining the team put together for Agent Deshpande's investigation? It's all about this, isn't it?" she said.

"No, it's not! Rishi's missing and I think something happened to him!" he said.

"Nothing happened. But something will happen when he gets back and I'll do it!" she said.

"Please understand- "he started.

"Stay within your duty or else I'll have you transferred!" she warned.

"But- "he started again.

"Just leave!" she ordered.

He sighed, said nothing and left with disappointment.

Back to the top 50 in Chennai, Radhika and Natasha went on foot to the docks with an agent. There were mainly five jetties. All but one had boats tied to them. Near the last jetty to their left was a small office of the in charge of the dockyard.

"Hmm…I guess; we should start asking in the office." Said Natasha.

"You go while I take some pictures around here with her. Stall him a bit." Said the agent to her. "Can you do that?"

"Yes, I can." She said.

"Remember, we don't know whether he's in on it too or not." Said Radhika.

"Yeah, I got it! You finish quickly!" said Natasha and left.

Radhika started walking around and taking pictures in one direction and the agent went in another direction doing the same while asking around.

Near an abandoned looking alley, on the left of the road, a pothole was open with the lid next to it. Inside was a ladder on which Indira and Aakash climbed down and jumped into the knee-deep sewage river. They both turned on their torches and started wading. Three to four more agents were doing the same in other holes nearby the area of the hotel.

"This is disgusting!" said Aakash with his complaining attitude, while they were walking.

"We can't go further. Look at the wall over there. It's completely shut!" said Indira.

"What do you mean? If it's shut, then how can the sewage go further? The sewage purification plant is on the other side of this part of the city." Said Aakash.

"Here!" – giving her hand – "I'll show you!" she said.

"No! They're dirtier than mine!" he said, refusing with disgust.

"Then when you fall, do not blame me!" she said.

"Okay, fine!" he said and held her hand.

They slowly waded closer to the wall.

"See closer!" – pointing downwards – "An automated shutter is placed. It can be opened from the sewage control but we have to check out the schedule. Even if it is opened, there is only half a foot gap but from far, you will think it's not there. Nobody can fit through there." Said Indira.

"What if she's very thin?" He asked.

"Then still, you can't expect her to go through the fast current of sewage with her crates and make it to the docks alive." She said.

"Yeah, good point." He said.

"Come on! Let's go back to the warehouse. I've taken enough pictures. After that, we'll call up Major Pal." Said Indira.

They started wading back when suddenly Aakash slips and falls in the sewage water!

"Oh gross!" he exclaimed with disgust.

Indira laughed.

"Shut up and pull me up!" he said.

She gave her hand while still laughing. He grabbed it firmly and suddenly pulled her down! She yelped and fell into the sewage next to him! That's when Aakash laughed.

"I'll kill you!" she said.

"Sorry, I couldn't help myself!" he said, still laughing.

She chuckled, sighed and looked at him. He stopped laughing and looked at her as well.

"What?" he asked.

"You just said sorry." She said.

A minute of silence occurred.

"You've changed." He said and she looked away. "It's a good thing!"

At that she looked back at him. There was a pause.

"Come on. Let's go!" she said.

They got up and waded carefully back to the pothole opening and climbed up the ladder out of the drain. They put the lid back on the pothole and left back to the warehouse.

A van arrived in the front of the hotel and parked. Two young boys had orange caps on with white t-shirts and jeans. They entered the hotel and were stopped by security. They lifted their arms while the security checked them with metal scanners. After that, they went to the basement and went down the stairs to a small room. Two security guards were there, one being overweight and another not that much. The two young boys took off their caps and revealed to be Arjun and Gaurav. In the van were two agents watching keenly. Arjun showed a business card of the company of the CCTV cameras. The security nodded and got up then left the room. Gaurav sat down in front of a computer controlling the cameras. All screens were blank showing "No Signal" on each screen. Gaurav inserted a pen drive. On the screen, it showed a small window opening showing a task saying "5 minutes to installation." And a loading sign.

Simran was at the hotel reception talking to the assistant manager and a police officer regarding the schedule with Major Pal talking to the receptionists at the front desks just behind her.

"I swear, madam, you look quite young to be an officer!" said the assistant manager.

"You can never tell one's age by looking, you know. And you've spoken with my superior right there. I just need four of my guys to go in the banquet." Said Simran.

"Yes, I can allow that. I have openings for three waiters and one bartender. Take it or leave it!" said the assistant manager.

"I'll take it." Said Simran.

"They have to come by 4:00 for preparation in the afternoon tomorrow. Then they can go back, get ready and arrive through the employee entrance." Said the officer.

"They'll be there." Said Simran.

"Oh! Here! Their IDs are here!" – giving three cards – "Make sure they are on time please." Said the assistant manager.

"Of course!" she said, took the cards and shaking hands with both.

"All right, I've got work now!" said the assistant manager and left.

"Thanks, sir!" said Simran to the officer.

"No problem. I've got orders and I've completed them. Anything else you'd like?" he asked.

"No, we've got everything we need." Said Major Pal.

They then left in a jeep and to the warehouse. After entering, Simran went and opened her laptop and saw a task window open saying "Installation complete." She opened an icon. Gaurav called her as it was written the same on the surveillance computer.

"Did you get it?" he asked.

"Yup." – while typing something and pressing enter – "All right. Your cameras are fixed. Now get out of there." Said Simran and cut the phone call.

Just then, Aakash and Indira arrived at the warehouse.

"Oh, my god! That stinks!" Simran exclaimed at looking at them covering her nose.

"What did you expect? This is the last time you ever make me do something like this!" said Aakash.

"I'm sorry. He needed eyes down there." Said Simran.

"Go wash up then tell me what you've found. Okay?" said Major Pal.

They nodded and left.

At the hotel surveillance room, the cameras regained their signals and showed the various halls and places of the hotel. Gaurav pulled out the pen drive and got up and went outside with Arjun.

"It's fixed. No need to worry." Said Arjun to the security and they left.

They went out of the hotel building and entered their waiting van. Immediately they left and returned to the warehouse quickly.

During the time while the cameras were down, Nikhil was taking pictures of the corridors dressed the same as Arjun and Gaurav. Raghav was looking around at the terrace.

At the warehouse, one by one, everybody arrived, gave their camera to Simran and went to freshen up and eat the food that an agent had brought back. Everybody sat down and ate except Simran. She was busy looking through the pictures, loading them and forming a holographic imagery of most of the area and formulating a plan. Radhika came over.

"Did you eat?" she asked.

"Yeah, I and Major Pal finished. You?" she asked.

"Yeah." Said Radhika.

Everyone was asleep when Simran suddenly woke up at 2:35 am to a few whispers in an adjoining room.

"Rules? You've got to be kidding me." Said Nikhil, inside.

"It's already bad enough that we have to listen to Simran. That Pal guy as well." said Raghav.

"Shut up, man! We just have to listen or else we can't get closure on Prakash!" whispered Aakash, annoyed.

I just went in the sewer because Indu did...why is Simran pairing us up?

He stopped at that.

"First thing is that if you show any objection, then I have the Director's number etched into my mind. And next, every order here will be initiated by me. Got it?" said Raghav, imitating Major Pal.

"Loud and clear!" said Arjun.

Everyone gave him a look as he entered the door.

"You all should be sleeping." He said.

"What do you want, Arjun?" asked Aakash.

"If I can hear you from the next room, so can everybody else. Including the agents on night duty. Consider yourself grateful and go to sleep." Said Arjun, sternly.

"I can't believe you're my friend." Said Raghav.

"Last time I checked, we were never friends. I don't care about what your problems are and I never did. I just want some results out of this so I'm obeying anybody." Said Arjun.

So, that's why…

Simran thought. Suddenly a sound from the opposite direction came and she heard footsteps. She checked around the warehouse then went to the roof. She saw Indira sitting quietly looking over the city. She climbed and sat next to her.

"What are you doing here?" asked Indira.

"The boys were ranting about me and Major Pal. I can't help it." said Simran, crossing her legs.

"Forget them." She said.

"You have to sleep. Major Pal won't want mistakes. I don't think any of us do." Said Simran.

"I haven't slept in a few days. I usually have this problem." She said.

"How come?"

"Let's leave it at nightmares…"

"Would you feel offended if I asked why you kept going home?"

"No, I wouldn't. I have a lot of reasons to go home. Mostly just to help around because my dad is kind of sick. Sorry, you've got a lot on your mind about tomorrow, don't you?"

"I'm worried about you. Aakash is distracting your work at school, I mean. And not duty but studies." Said Simran.

Indira said nothing.

"What really happened with him?" asked Simran.

A pause occurred.

"I was always weak, you know? From class 8, I was always bullied. I always fainted because I never ate well. Everybody thought I was weak, and so I did. Do you know how that feels?" She asked.

Simran frowned but paid attention closely.

"You don't know much about the school. The students are terrible till class 10. But as soon as you go to class 11, nobody can touch you. I always felt terrible but as soon as I finished school, I trained. It was hard…" She said, letting down a tear and wiping it away immediately.

"Then what about Aakash?" asked Simran.

"We went out in class 9 for just a few months. But he was like everybody else. When they made fun of me, he laughed too. He insulted me, he always picked on me. Now, nobody makes fun of me anymore but he is right there. Always pissing me off. I was determined for the top 400, though. I guess, that was why." She said.

Simran said nothing.

"I don't know…should I kill him for that or thank him for making me qualify as top 50? I can never forgive him. And now…he doesn't get lost. I don't know how to handle him. At least now, no matter how much he tries, he can't make me angry that much." She said, sighing.

A pause occurred.

"If he never cared about you, he would've left you alone. Did he? No. He didn't let you out of his sight. I'm sure he did it to help you. I guess, he wanted you to break up with him." Said Simran.

"Maybe so." She said.

"It's been a while since then, right? Like maybe two years. And drastic changes have occurred in our lives in two years.I'm not saying to get back together but can't you forgive him?" she asked.

"I don't know if I can. I'm so weak inside no matter how strong I am." She said.

"But it's a good opportunity now, for everybody to try to get along. We only have another year to go. Should we just waste time in anger or fulfil our duty well?" asked Simran.

"Yeah, you're right. So, what to do?" asked Indira.

"First, you go sleep. When you get up tomorrow, you'll be able to decide better. Okay?" said Simran, giving a small smile of reassurance.

She looked at her in surprise and nodded.

"Why are you helping me? You put us together today. Why should you care about what happens between us?" She asked.

"I don't know. Personally, the only thing that matters to me is that we all cooperate more. Don't tell anyone this." Said Simran.

Indira looked at her with a newfound respect.

"You're a sucker for relationships, just like everybody else. Aren't you?" said Indira.

"Think what you like." She said.

They went downstairs to their beds and went to sleep.

Chapter Five – On the lookout...

Back to the school, Siddharth went walking to his hostel room after coming out of the Principal's cabin. He was deep in thought.

I need to go! I need to check the town! Right now, I think I'm allowed because of the timings. But I need someone with me to cover more area. But who? I don't trust anybody. Gaurav won't get back until day after tomorrow. Hmm...what about

Priya? Oh, there she is! I'll get her to help me without telling
everything.

"Hey! Priya! Wait up!" called out Siddharth, going after her.

She stopped and turned around.

"Oh, you. Yeah, what's up?" she asked.

"I need your help. I have to go the nearby town to search for
anything out of the blue right now!" he said.

"I can't come. I have too many things to complete. If I go
with you, I'll have to stay up all night completing them. Go
with Neerav!" she said.

"Come on! We've only got an hour! It's important to go
now!" he said.

"Go with Neerav!" she said and left.

Where will I go looking for him now?!

Siddharth took out his phone from his pocket and called up
Neerav, who was in his room completing his gadget log file
when he picked up.

"Yeah, tell me!" said Neerav.

"I need your help! Get down to the parking lot now! It's important and we only have an hour!" said Siddharth.

"Huh? What- "started Neerav.

"Come down to the parking lot right now!" said Siddharth and cut the call.

What's so important?

He gets up and puts his file in his drawer. He then puts on a jacket, ties his shoes on and grabs his phone putting it in his pocket. Then he goes down after locking his door. He reaches the parking and finds Siddharth waiting on a bike.

"Where are you going?" asked Neerav.

"The correct question is where are we going!" he replied.

"Tell me!" he said.

"Get on! I'll tell you everything on the way!" he said.

Neerav gets on the bike behind Siddharth and they left out the gates towards the highway and drove for a while.

In the warehouse, everybody assembled around Simran. She presses a button on her tablet. Just then, a holographic image of the area appeared in neon blue. The image was three dimensional with every single detail. At seeing that everybody was astonished.

I feel so useless…such a show off!

Nikhil thought.

"All right! Gather around! Listen carefully." Said Major Pal.

"How'd you do all this?" asked Aakash.

"You can ask about that later. We don't have much time." Said Arjun, standing right next to Simran.

"Arjun's right. Continue, sir!" said Indira.

Everyone gave a look to her then looked back at Arjun and Simran.

"The police confirmed that Lu is here. She arrived a while ago and she's staying at a different hotel. Two officers are staking out nearby and will inform me directly if anything's up. The plan is simple and it will stay that way. No deviating." Said Major Pal, sternly.

Nobody said anything.

"First up, the target will be going to the banquet at any time from 9:00pm onwards and we all can't be in the banquet. I've got four IDs. Three for waiters and one for a bartender. Radhika, you are a waiter!" – handing over an ID – "Nikhil and Natasha, you are waiters as well." – handing over the IDs – "Ma'am, here's yours." – handing an ID to the agent that had scoured the docks with Radhika and Natasha – "You need to be at the hotel by 4:00pm sharp tomorrow for some little instructions. And you'll have to stay for the entire banquet to avoid suspicion. Aakash and Indira, you two are on the terraces of the hotel and adjoining buildings with at least a few agents and police personnel. Arjun and I will be in the streets with Major Pal, Major Pal will keep roaming on a bike and us on foot, roaming the area with a few police officers. We'll keep checking the docks. Lastly, Gaurav and Raghav, you two have to search the hotel. Mostly for the shipment. Got it?" said Simran.

"Woah, wait! I'm not being with this guy! No way!" said Gaurav.

"Same here! Put me as a waiter!" said Raghav.

"Shut up!!" shouted Major Pal and his voice echoed in the hall making it louder and fierce.

They both became silent.

"Gaurav, come here." Said Simran.

He walked forward. She put her arm around his shoulder and pulled him to a corner.

"Choose quickly. If you don't partner up with him, he'll be around Radhika and I don't like that. I and Arjun must be together, Aakash and Indira too. For now, Nikhil and Natasha will be in the banquet together because I don't want them apprehending the target. So, do you want to deal with Raghav or make Radhika deal with him? Do you want this to work or not?" Simran slowly explained, while whispering.

Shit…she's right…

"Okay, fine!" said Gaurav.

"Okay, as soon as you find the shipment, get it, take pictures of it and if there's anything wrong, I'll call you up." She said.

"You mean if there is anything wrong with Arjun?" he said.

"Not just him." She said.

They went back to the table and Major Pal explained further details of the plan.

"Hey, Prakash. She must be reaching by now. Should I call her?"

Prakash was brooding from a balcony of his hotel room in Paris when he turned around to see Brad.

"No need. I'll call her in a bit. She needs to scour the situation." He replied.

"Not being rude but we have to know about the forces there." Said Brad, walking over and sitting down on a chair then lifted his feet on the small table.

Prakash still stood there watching the scenery of traffic and the Eiffel Tower in the distance all lit up.

"The hacker man Dean is having a hard time decrypting codes to find that IP address. It's even more protected than army networks." Said Brad, lighting a cigarette.

"Are any of our dealers missing or dead?" asked Prakash.

"Nope. All alive and ready for their deliveries. Are there better hackers than Dean?" he asked back.

"Even if there were, they would be private, not from intelligence." He said.

A pause. Brad exhaled an amount of smoke and relaxed.

"We suffered a lot of heavy losses. What in the hell were you thinking?!" said Brad. "You're lucky that customers still have faith in Kapoor enterprise."

Prakash said nothing and just continued to watch the traffic below the hotel.

"You listening to me?" asked Brad.

"I'm going to call her now." Said Prakash, taking out his phone and dialling a number while walking back inside the room.

Siddharth and Neerav reached the nearby town and parked near the railway station.

"You go check out that side where the bakery, hardware shop and the electrical shop is. I'll check out these three alleys. Check under the buildings and don't forget the terraces too." Said Siddharth.

"Got it. We'll meet back here later!" said Neerav and they split up.

Neerav went enquiring at the bakery first, finding no answer. He couldn't go upstairs either. He next tried the hardware shop obtaining the same answer. He went over to the pet shop but found it closed. He looked around him then sneaked behind to check.

Siddharth checked in the first alley and found nothing. He went over to the second one where there was a bar and enquired at the counter.

"We're not open and…wait! You are under age." Said the bartender.

"I'm not here to buy anything. I have a friend!" – showing his phone in which a picture of Rishi was there – "Have you seen him?" asked Siddharth.

"I didn't see him here but outside the bar. He was just roaming on the streets and he met a trio. They are my customers, normal businessmen, always going together. I don't know anything else." He said.

"It's okay. Thank you!" said Siddharth and left.

He went to the terrace of the bar building and could see all the other terraces but still couldn't find anything. He goes down and checks the third alley but still nothing was found. He sighs and goes to the main road, crosses it and sees Neerav coming towards him.

"Any luck?" asked Siddharth.

"No, what about you?" asked Neerav.

"I got nothing so far. That coffee shop is the last place here." Said Siddharth.

"Let's go, then!" said Neerav.

They both went inside the coffee shop and directly went to the lady at the counter.

"Hello auntie!" greeted Neerav.

"Oh hello! What will it be today? Coffee or cake?" she greeted back.

"Nothing actually. Have you seen our friend Rishi anywhere?" asked Siddharth.

"Uh, no! Not quite. I was looking forward to seeing him. I wanted to give my condolences. Anything happened?" she asked.

"No, just asking." Said Siddharth.

"Some kids were playing outside and their ball fell on your terrace. Can we go get it?" asked Neerav.

"Yeah, be back quickly, though!" she said.

With that excuse, they quickly sprinted up the stairs at the back and opened the door to the terrace. As soon as it did, they got the shock of their lives at what was seen in the corner! Siddharth suddenly covered his nose at the horrible stench. Neerav was too shocked to do anything and fell on his knees with tears pouring down from his face!

"No! No! No!" Neerav wailed, while covering his nose.

Chapter Six – He's dead! Plan in action!

Rishi's body lay there in the corner lifeless.

After an hour, a crowd was formed on that terrace with the Principal and a few local police officers. Lines were drawn around the body while a few officers were examining the crime scene.

"I'm telling the truth! I barely go to the terrace of my shop! I don't know anything about this!" said the lady of the coffee shop to the officer questioning her.

Siddharth was holding Neerav in his arms while Neerav was still shedding tears. The head Inspector came to the Principal, who was standing near them with her hands folded, and showed a file. She turned it down.

"In a hurry, I forgot my glasses." She said.

He nodded.

"The body was found by those two with three bullets in it. Two bullets in chest and one in forehead. Cleanly done with a service type pistol. Bullets found were .22 long rifle. Body is at least a day old. Further can be said after the autopsy. Anything you need, madam?" asked the Inspector after stating.

"No media coverage please. I will inform my superiors and the family of the deceased. I'll handle the students. Clear up everything quickly. Understood?" instructed the Principal. He nodded and left. She turned to Siddharth and Neerav.

"So, you were looking for him…" she said.

They both said nothing and just looked at her.

"Do you know anything about who did this? Do any of you know more about this?" she asked.

"No…" said Siddharth.

"Start finding some clues on your own then. Be warned that we are being targeted. Either us or the LOCKER so keep alert." She said.

They both still said nothing and tears were still coming out of Neerav.

"Get a hold of yourself, Agent Sharma." Said the Principal. Neerav sniffled once and wiped his tears. He stood up and dusted himself.

"We have a lot of work to do, understood? So, it's important that you'll have to make do with it. I'm enforcing more changes and you will obey. Understood?" said the Principal, sternly.

"Yes, ma'am." They replied.

"I'll talk to the director later. Go back to school and give the news and my instructions to the rest of the agents. Now." She said.

"Yes, ma'am." They said and left.

They drove back to school and parked the bike. Before going to duty, Siddharth told everyone in the meeting room.

Neerav was in his room and didn't come for duty. Later, Shreya went up to Neerav's room and stayed there.

I'll tell the top 50 later because their mission is tomorrow.

Siddharth had decided.

The next day, Simran woke up early and went out of the warehouse to a nearby tea shop and bought many small cups of tea with a biscuit packet back. She entered and put them on the table. Just then, she got a call from the officers at the target's hotel telling her to meet them at the police station in a few minutes. She quickly tore a piece of paper, scribbled something on it and left. She met the two officers at the police station and they all sat down in a room. Major Pal was also there.

"We tapped her room phone. She was having a conversation with someone. Listen carefully." Said one officer.

He pressed play on the recorder.

"Hello?" said one voice, receiving a call.

"This is the target." Said the officer and let it continue.

"Reached the place safely?" asked one deep voice one end.

It instantly seemed familiar to Simran. She listened more keenly.

"Yes, I'm here. I've got the shipment located and it's safely there." Said the target.

"Good. Remember. No screw ups. We need that money for our project coming up." Said the voice.

"Yes, of course. It'll get done. I'll meet you soon." She said.

"Looking forward to it." Said the voice and the call ended.

The officer pressed the stop button and gave her the recorder. She took it.

"Anything at all?" asked Major Pal.

She frowned.

"Let's continue with our job now." He said and they left.

At the warehouse, everyone was up and ready. They went down and found Simran's note saying "Tea and biscuits. I went to check a few arrangements with sir. Be back soon to revise the plan." They started sipping their tea by the time she came back.

Simran was at the far end of the street in which their warehouse was located on the phone with the LSS Director.

"Keep the tape with you, Agent Khanna. It will be safe." She said.

"Why?" asked Simran.

"Prakash has people keeping a very clear watch on me and the IB. As far as we know, he thinks that you're dead. So it'll be with you." She said.

There still might be people inside the agency working for him...I have no choice.

"But Major Pal has it." she said.

"I'll tell him to give it to you. He's only brought for this mission. The case is yours." Said the Director.

"Okay." She said.

"Good. Remember, we need the target more than the shipment. And be careful with her. She's an excellent fighter." Said the Director.

"Understood." Said Simran.

The call ended.

Major Pal handed the drive to her and they went back inside the warehouse. Everybody gathered around and they revised the plan. When it turned around 3:45 pm, Radhikha, Nikhil, Natasha with an Agent left with their IDs to the hotel for their preparations and the rest of them discussed further details of their duties.

Meanwhile, at school, an officer was in the Principal's cabin. The LSS Director had sent him.

"In Agent Aggarwal's body, there was only one bullet hole straight through his heart. The bullet was found somewhere near him. It was a .22 long rifle. And that made us suspicious enough because a few top 400 agents that were killed a few weeks ago, their bodies are still preserved. We checked their files again. All of them were shot in different places but at least there was a .22 long rifle bullet in them." Said the officer.

"I see…" she replied. "Why do you think the same type of bullets were used?"

"I don't know…" he said, placing a packet on the table containing the bullet.

She picked it up and examined it. As she turned the bullet, something caught her eye and shocked her.

Kapoor enterprise?! Prakash got him killed?!

"The murder investigations of every top 400 agent are taken over by the LSS Director. So, if any information is worth saying, it should be informed to her. Convey this message to the agents." He said.

"Did the director notice this? This shows who ordered the hit!" Said the Principal.

"Yes, she has. We are investigating and on the search for him still." He said.

"I see…" she replied. "Thank you."

At the warehouse, Gaurav received a call from Siddharth.

"Yeah, everything is fine here. Your side?" asked Gaurav.

"So so…I've heard that every top 400 murder case is under the Director. And if we get anything relevant we have to tell her." Said Siddharth.

"Hmm…so far we don't know anything. Did you try for the extra checking permission?" asked Gaurav.

"She wasn't understanding the gravity of the situation. Sorry. Maybe we can go during the normal timings." He replied.

"Yeah, if only that is possible then fine. What about Rishi?" asked Gaurav.

"Uh…" he hesitated.

"Gaurav, we have to go now!" Simran called from outside.

"Hold that. I need to go now. I'll get back and ask later. Bye!" said Gaurav and cut the call.

Shit…that was close…

Siddharth thought.

"Gaurav, we don't have much time! Let's go!" said Simran.

They all went out with their things and locked the warehouse. They walked till the main road and split up from there. Aakash and Indira went in an adjoining building with a couple of officers and went to the terrace. From there they all leapt onto other adjoining terraces spreading out. Gaurav and Raghav entered the hotel and split up. Arjun and Simran stood on the street connecting the hotel and the docks. The officers mostly spread out near the hotel. None were near the docks to avoid being spotted but Major Pal kept roaming on his bike.

"Everyone's in position at the terraces." Said Aakash, informing.

"We're in the hotel and still searching." Gaurav updated.

"The banquet started and there are a lot of people here." Said Radhika at the bar in the hotel function hall.

"Still no sign of target." Said Nikhil while serving a few drinks to people.

"Don't get hasty, guys. She'll be here." Said Major Pal.

It became 9:45…still no sign of her…it became 10:13 when she finally arrived.

"Target entered the hall! She's wearing a dull sky-blue dress. She only has a tiny purse with her." Said the agent at the banquet, while serving a drink to a customer.

"All right. Keep your eyes on her." Said Major Pal.

After a few minutes, messages were received.

"I've got the shipment location. It's in the basement of the hotel." Said Raghav.

"Pictures?" asked Simran.

"Yeah, got them." He said.

"Wait, I've got another two crates here that could be the shipment as well." Said Gaurav.

"Well…that's kind of bad. How do we solve this?" asked Aakash.

"Yeah, which one is the real one?" asked Arjun.

"She did this to trick us…most likely there might be a lot of them here…" said Radhika, while pouring a drink for a customer.

"Sir, give us orders." Said Gaurav.

Simran looked at her watch. It was 10:20. She thought deeply.

"Sir?" called out an agent.

Major Pal did not reply.

"We got 10 minutes. Raghav, you stay near the one in the basement. Gaurav, I've sent a few officers inside. All of you spread out and check for more boxes. Measure the dimensions. Only the ones that are heavy. Now! Major Pal is with us, his earpiece got spoilt!" said Simran.

"Got it!" said Gaurav.

"What about me?" asked Raghav.

"I've got doubts on that one! Stay there." Said Simran.

Plus, she's about to make a move now...

After a couple of minutes, it was 10:24.

"I've got a couple more boxes. Each are of different heights." Said Gaurav.

"How does she plan on getting the shipment to them? The drop is almost there and she didn't leave yet." Said Arjun to Major Pal, who had parked his bike and waited with them.

"Keep alert!" said Simran. "Indira! Aakash!"

"Yeah!" they said.

"Do not underestimate her! She can make weapons. She might have some concealable ones with her." Warned Simran.

"So, what should we do, Miss know it all?" asked Aakash, getting annoyed.

"Shoot her leg or arm and tie her up. No fights. It won't end well. Got it?" Simran instructed.

"Yes!" they said.

"Don't dare call me that again, Aakash!" said Simran.

"Whatever!" he said.

Indira was at an adjoining terrace of the hotel with a few agents, thinking.

She's one person…we have many people with us. Simran's worrying too much.

Meanwhile, Aakash was on the terrace of the hotel thinking.

No sign yet…

Suddenly a message came to everybody's ears at 10:28!

"Target left the banquet hall!" said Radhika.

"She went upstairs!" said Natasha.

Aakash loaded his gun and so did five other agents and police.

"In position." An agent said.

The officers spread while he waited near the door in the shadow for her. The target moved stealthily up the stairs with her purse. It was unusual but she had no gun with her. She reached the last few stairs and the terrace door. She opened it, stepped outside and closed the door. As soon as she turned around, the five officers were surrounding her. Behind her came Aakash with his gun pointed at her.

"Hands up." – she did so without a word – "Purse! Hand it over!" said the head agent.

She lifted it up but dropped it on the ground by accident. She bent down to pick it up when suddenly she kicked Aakash behind her and punched and officer in front of her at the same time! Aakash fell back dropping his gun! So did the officer in front of him! She attacked the other three in front of her by suddenly pulling a small knife-like ring and piercing various places with it. They howled with pain! The officer she punched first came attacking but she pierced him in his chest! He fell dead instantly. She immediately was continuously kicking and punching two agents simultaneously. One agent landed a few punches at her but she was too fast!

Aakash came running and kicked her from the back! She staggered but stood erect. Aakash punched her again and she staggered again. As he was about to punch her again, she grabbed his fist with one hand and kicked him in the stomach. She cut his face and pierced his thigh. He howled in pain before falling! She wipes a drop of blood off her face and ran away!

"She's getting…away!" Aakash yelled.

Chapter Seven – Mission completed?

Indira suddenly hears shouts!

What was that?!

She loaded her gun and waited in a corner. The others were spread out on the buildings in wait of her. After a moment, she saw the target sprinting in her direction.

What the hell?! What happened to the others?! Shit!

The target landed and Indira was behind her. Just as she landed, Indira shot a bullet in her leg! She yelped and staggered. She fell on her knees dropping her ring. Indira went closer while pointing her gun. Just as she was a foot away, Lu saw her shadow. Lu immediately pulled a very sleek sword from her dress, got up, turned around and cut her arm twice leaving her deep wounds! She slit once on her other arm! Indira screamed in pain and fell on her knees but still held her gun at her! Lu slit her gun in half! She limped away while Indira got up and threw her gun away.

"Hey!!!!" the top 50 agent shouted out.

At that the target stopped limping away and turned around to face her.

I can't let her go! I will have to fight!

"You are not going anywhere!!" she said.

"In what state are you in to tell me that, huh?" the target calmly replied.

She was just about to turn around to go when she stopped and turned around at what the little brave agent said.

"Bring it. I'll fight you." She said.

The target laughed out loud in the shrillest voice which was really annoying to hear.

"Don't you fear for your life, kid?" she asked, in amusement.

"Nice weapon you got there." Said the agent.

"It's my creation. It can cut through anything!" she said.

"You only have your weapons to save you...or else you'd be dead." Said the agent.

"Even if that was true...my death wouldn't be by your hand!" said the target.

"Want to bet on that?" the agent taunted.

"Come on then!" – throwing her sword down – "Anytime now!" she said and took a stance.

They both ran to each other and attacked! Lu landed a punch on Indira's face and a kick in her stomach but Indira retaliated with a punch on her face! Lu punched her face and Indira punched hard on her stomach! She then kicked her and Lu staggered but stood erect and punched Indira's face again! Lu then leaped high and kicked her face hard that made Indira fall hitting the ground!

Indira couldn't get up. Lu picked her up and threw her! She almost fell off the roof if she hadn't caught the ledge! Lu came and looked down.

"You won't hold on for long, kid!" she said and left.

"Ah! She's headed to the docks!" Indira yelled.

"Let's go!" said Simran to Arjun and Major Pal. "The Docks!"

They started running with a few officers towards the docks.

"The shipment! Simran! Ah!" screamed Indira, still holding onto the ledge.

"What?!" she asked, still running.

"The one in the basement- "she started.

"Simran! The shipment! A floor opened and the crate fell down below! There is sewage below!" said Raghav.

"Get to the drains, Raghav!" said Simran. "The rest of you go too!"

The officers left and went to all the potholes. They pulled up the lids and entered them. Arjun and Simran kept running to the docks with Major Pal. Gaurav came out of the hotel and went running after them.

Meanwhile, Indira was still hanging from the ledge of the building.

"Agent Jaiswal! What happened to your men?!" asked an agent.

"They are dead, sir! Just get her!" said Indira.

"Indu, what happened?!" exclaimed Nikhil, from a storage closet.

"I'm hanging on the edge! I'm going to die!" Indira screamed.

"Somebody get to her! Anybody!" shouted Simran.

"I can't hold on! Ah! Help!" Indira screamed. "I can't hold… any longer!"

She left her hand from the ledge but Aakash reached in time to grab her hand, preventing her from falling!

"Don't you dare give up on me!" he said, firmly catching hold of her hand.

She pulled herself up and he helped. She climbed over the ledge and sat down next to him breathing a sigh of relief.

"There's blood here. Were you shot?" he asked.

"I shot her. She cut me." She said, breathing heavily. "You?"

"She cut me too. One of my guys are dead, the rest are wounded...I heard you scream so I somehow came!" he said, panting.

"Thank goodness!" Natasha said.

"Go back to the warehouse, you two! Clean your wounds!" said Simran, sending a message, while running.

"Sorry we couldn't get her!" said Aakash.

"It's okay! Major Pal said to just go!" said Simran.

"Okay?! How's it okay?! She got away! She cut my leg and Indu's arm and threw her off the roof and- "he started.

"He what?! You were on the edge of a building?!" exclaimed Radhika.

"Calm down, guys!" said Simran.

"Yeah she did! I came in time!" said Aakash.

"That's good. Look, we're reaching the docks. You go back to the warehouse now! Who knows how deep those cuts are!" said Simran.

Gaurav reached a few metres behind Simran, Major Pal and Arjun as they ran. They finally reached the docks and stopped. They looked around and couldn't see anything.

"Is the deal done?" asked Gaurav, catching up to them.

"I think the deal's off…" said Major Pal.

They kept looking around. Suddenly Arjun caught sight of Lu jumping down from a building to a small roof of another building then jumping down landing badly because of her limp. She starts running towards a speedboat when Arjun, Gaurav and Major Pal run towards her. Simran stopped to receive a message from Raghav.

"Simran, we've acquired the shipment!" he said.

"Keep it safe!" she said.

She ran behind them on the docks when she stopped and noticed the damp wooden bridge. She bent, pressed her hand quickly on the wet wood and smelled it.

Kerosene!!

Simran got up and saw Lu stop while they kept running towards her. She took out a lighter, lit it and dropped it on the ground!

"STOP! Stop running!!" Simran screamed.

As soon as it dropped, the wooden planks that made the jetties were all set ablaze spontaneously! The fire burned so fiercely! Major Pal stopped and shielded himself with his arms. Arjun and Gaurav stopped and fell back on the ground! While indirectly shielding Gaurav, Arjun's pant caught fire! Gaurav pulled him farther from the fire and Simran took off her jacket and started to put out the fire on his leg. Major Pal rushed over and used his jacket as well! It extinguished but left burns on his skin! Lu, in the meantime, jumped into the boat, revved it up and sped away!

Dammit!

Simran panted. Arjun yelped in pain while grabbing his leg! Gaurav breathed heavily while watching the fire still there. "Target missed. Sorry, guys." Said Simran and disconnected.

Indira and Aakash had reached the warehouse first. They went inside and sat down with the first aid kit. Indira fixes Aakash's wounds first.

"Ah! It hurts!" he said. "Please stop! Ah! Enough!"

"Then do it yourself!" she said, getting fed up.

"Fine, just do it!" he said.

She finished wiping the blood and started bandaging.

"Lift your leg up. Just for a second!" she said.

He did so and she wrapped the bandage around the wound.

"Done!" she said.

"Okay, your turn!" he said.

She sits down on the table and he started wiping her wounds.

"Tell me if it hurts." He said.

"It doesn't." she said.

"Yeah it does."

"Whatever…"

"Don't act so tough."

"I'm not acting."

"Yeah, you are."

"You just have to have a problem with everything, don't you?"

"You just have to prove how better you are than me, don't you?"

"Don't change the subject."

"Almost done…" he said.

She didn't reply. He finished bandaging her.

"I'll take you to a hospital when we get back." He said.

"There's no need to-" she started.

"I don't care. Besides, you have to get better or your family will keep asking questions on your next visit."

"Don't act like you care on what my family thinks."

"Of course I do. I always did care."

"I know."

"No, you don't because-wait! You know?" he asked, surprised.

She looked up and nodded.

"Simran helped me realize it. You fooled me well. I feel like such an idiot." she said.

He said nothing and looked down. She got down from the table in slight pain and started limping to her room.

"You still mad at me?" Aakash asked, not turning around.

"Obviously." she said.

Just then, Raghav entered the warehouse. After a while, Nikhil, Natasha and Radhika arrived. They all went to go change and freshen up. Arjun was breathing heavily when

Gaurav and Simran carried him to the warehouse. After they dressed his wounds, they entered a small room without being noticed and closed the door. Gaurav and Arjun stayed on the ground. Arjun's head was on Gaurav's lap.

"I'll be back!" said Simran and left outside to meet everyone. They were all standing there.

They all hate me more now…

"Aakash and Indu…are you two okay?" she asked.

"We're good." Said Aakash.

"I'll be fine." Said Indira, being supported by Radhika.

"Raghav, did you hand over the shipment?" she asked.

"Yes, it's going to the CBI. We'll get details later." He said.

"Well…Major Pal said 'bye' and left to tend to his agents…" – putting an envelope on the table – "Our tickets for tomorrow's flight are here. It's at 3:30am. Sleep well." she said.

"That's it? Are we not going to worry about what will happen?" asked Natasha.

"We've failed the mission! What will we tell the Director?!" asked Nikhil.

"We only failed half of it. Don't make such a big deal." Said Radhika.

"We're going to get screwed. I will make a big deal." Said Nikhil.

"Shut up, man! We tried our best!" said Raghav.

"It's of no use saying that because she got away!" said Nikhil.

"What did you say?" asked Aakash going near him. "It's of no use, you say?"

"You, Simran, should have put me out there. I could've nabbed her. You purposely put me in the banquet. You told that Pal to!" Said Nikhil.

"You think these cuts on my body means nothing?! You think her throwing Indu off a building means nothing?! You think you can do a better job at leading the mission than Simran can?!" asked Aakash, angrily.

"And if I say yes, then?" asked Nikhil, taunting him.

Aakash grabbed him by the shirt firmly when Radhika and Indira pulled him back. Natasha pulled back Nikhil.

"I'm not in the mood to deal with you. I've got other things to take care of. Indu, go to the left room and sleep. Natasha, please get everybody up and ready tomorrow. Pack up. Good night!" said Simran.

Natasha nodded and left. Everybody else did. Aakash was about to go when Simran stops him.

"I'm sorry...but Arjun got burnt in the fire and she got away. I'm so sorry you two got hurt." She said.

"It's okay, Agent Khanna. Good night." He said and left.

Simran went back to the small room where Gaurav sat with Arjun. Indira entered as well and saw Arjun in pain as well. She stared at him for a while then went and lied down on a mat in a corner. Within a minute, she slept.

"Switch with me." Said Gaurav.

Simran sat down in his place and put Arjun's head on her lap.

"I'll check for pillows." He said and left.

"What are you doing?" Arjun groaned while asking.

"Helping you." She replied.

"Why?"

"Well, we're partners, aren't we?"

"Seriously?"

"Sorry, I almost broke my promise…"

"How did you carry me?"

"Gaurav helped."

"Shit…"

"Don't make such a big deal. Be happy it was him. He's trustable."

"You trust him?"

"I didn't say that!"

"Yeah, you'll never trust anybody, will you?"

There was a pause.

"Feeling comfortable?" she asked.

"Yeah, I am. I'll sleep now. Tell Gaurav that a pillow is not required." He said.

"Don't sleep yet or else you'll black out."

"Then talk to me. I'm bored."

"Go to sleep then. I hate you too much."

"Same here, Miss know it all. But we're already talking now."

She was silent.

"Sorry that we couldn't get her." He said.

"It's my fault. I didn't expect her to be this good." She said.

"No, I screwed up again. I let her get away. Then she set the entire dockyard on fire!" he said.

"It's okay…" she said, feeling his forehead and neck to check for a fever.

"What'll happen now?" he asked.

"Well, you'll be fine. Pillows are not there. The four of us should stay here. I'll keep watch outside." Gaurav just came and said.

"Gaurav, take my place." Said Simran but noticed Arjun fast asleep already.

"I hate to break it to you but you'll have to stay like that. He'll be fine by tomorrow." He said.

Great, I'm spending the night with him again!

Simran awoke abruptly. She had been sleeping throughout the night in the same position with her back against the wall. Arjun wasn't there and she was alone. Even Indira left the room.

Ow…

Just then Radhika arrives.

"We're leaving in half an hour. Get ready!" she said and left. Everybody packed up their things and left the warehouse in a crammed-up taxi to the airport. They reached and checked into the flight gates. After entering the plane, everyone started settling down. Simran was unable to lift her bag to put it into the overhead storage without her neck hurting. Arjun just then arrived and put his bag up with no difficulty. He grabs hers and puts it right next to his then closes the storage.

"Thanks…" she said.

"Thanks for saving my life." He said.

"Your life or your reputation?" she asked.

He was silent.

"Don't mention it. And Gaurav carried you." She said.

He was still silent.

"What happened?" she asked.

"Nikhil made a big deal yesterday, huh?" he said.

"Oh yeah, Aakash was going to kill him." She said.

"Did he ask where I was?" he asked.

"Nope." She said and left ahead.

Just then Arjun got a text on his phone showing "I don't like to be kept waiting. My order shouldn't take this long." from a private number. He sat down in his seat, looked around, checked Simran being away from sight then replied, "Meet me in our place at 10:00pm sharp."

After a few minutes, his phone buzzed. He again looked around and saw Nikhil and Gaurav sit down in their seats. He opened his message inbox and his new message saying "I don't do so late. Make it 5:00pm."

Dammit! Oh, come on! Should I send Nikhil-No! I'm owing a lot of favours already. And to even Simran!

"4:30pm. Final." Arjun replied. After a few minutes of waiting, his phone buzzed again. He immediately opened the message finding the Private number saying "Deal."

Aakash was standing in front of Simran. They saw Gaurav and Indira sitting together.

"Hey, Gaurav!" – he looked up – "Come sit with me!" she said while eying at Aakash.

"Surely!" he said and got up with his kindle in his hand.

He moved out and sat next to Simran in the seat ahead of them. Aakash sat down next to Indira.

"Hey." he said.

"I don't want you near me." She said.

"Look, I know you're mad about everything." he said.

"Oh, so smart." She said, sarcastically.

"I'm trying to apologize here. Would you let me?" He said.

She was silent.

"I'm sorry. Can we go back to how we were?" he asked.

She looked at him then looked away.

"I'm still mad at you…but you can take me to the hospital when we get back." She said.

He slightly smiled.

Their hands slowly held together. Simran and Gaurav noticed.

"Wow…that was cool." Said Gaurav.

"I know!" she said.

Chapter Eight – Clues and Suspicions...

"What?!"

Everybody was shocked during break time. The top 50 just heard the news on Rishi's murder from the rest of the agents. They all were in the meeting room.

"So..." – sitting down in shock – "he really was there." Said Simran.

"Yeah, he was." Said Neerav.

"Of course, he was. Why are you saying that?" asked Nikhil.

"Because Simran traced him." Said Gaurav.

"Siddharth and Neerav found him though." Said Simran.

"Think, if she had listened to you, we would've never found Rishi at all, Nikhil!" Said Natasha, this time, letting down a couple of tears.

"I…" he started.

"You've said enough. Just stop it." Said Aakash.

Nikhil left in anger. Natasha cried silently in Shreya's arms.

I can't believe this…

Simran thought.

"When and where was he found?" asked Gaurav.

"Day before yesterday evening at the coffee shop near the station." Said Siddharth.

Just before duty, Radhika received a call. She was with Simran in the corridor of their hostel floor.

"Yes?... What?!... For what?!... Are you sure?... But that was the place where-Oh...Got it." She said and cut the call.

"What happened?" asked Simran.

"I got to go. There's a bomb threat. Guess where!" said Radhika.

"Coffee shop where Rishi's body was found." Said Simran.

"Yup, Gaurav left a while ago to check." Said Radhika.

"Why there?"

"Someone's trying to erase something there. Go find out what." Said Simran.

She nodded and left. She reached the parking and got on a bike. She left and reached the highway. She reached the town after a while. She reaches the coffee shop and sees the door open. She goes inside. Gaurav was about to go outside the door when they crashed into each other and fell.

"Ah! What the hell- "started Gaurav.

"SHH!" Radhika said Closing his mouth.

There was silence for some time. Just then, they hear a faint beeping sound. They get up and look around the place. The beeping got louder and they saw a pack of dynamite with a timer. Another beeping came from another direction as well and it got louder.

"That's a…" Gaurav said.

"BOMB!!" Radhika shouted.

They quickly get up and run out the door. They keep running when the building blasted! They fell at a distance, got up and ran as fast as they could while covering their heads. There was fire and smoke everywhere. People scattered in various directions and ran away! The police arrived with the fire brigade and started extinguishing the fire. Gaurav and Radhika were in the street opposite the commotion and were catching their breath.

"Oh, my god! How did you know?! Why didn't you call me?!" exclaimed Gaurav.

"Do you think I didn't try?! You suddenly left, idiot! You should've waited!" said Radhika.

"A tip came after I left?" he asked.

"Believe me, just after you left, I got a call from a messenger about this!" said Radhika, panting.

"I can form a few conclusions because I found this." Said Gaurav, holding up two passports. "It was at a table. I don't know who these people are."

Radhika took them and checked.

"They seem familiar. Maybe Simran will remember. But tell your conclusions." She said.

"The building was scheduled for demolition a month from now. Erasing evidence was the bomber's priority. And I think the one who killed Aparna killed Rishi too. He must have found out something." Said Gaurav.

"Yeah. That's a good theory. Let's go back and tell Simran." She said and started walking.

"Radhika." Gaurav called out.

She stopped and turned around. He walked over and hugged her tightly. She was taken aback. He pulled away.

"Thank you." He said.

They both got on their bikes and left back to school. Arjun had just finished handing over a package to a person and had noticed the blast. He also saw Gaurav and Radhika leaving the street. After he saw them leave, he went to the blast site where a huge crowd gathered in shock.

But why? Auntie still did not shift the furniture in the building yet!

He went closer while everyone was still in shock and looking at the blast site when a police officer stopped him.

"What's your business here?" he asked.

"Sorry. The smell was weird." said Arjun, secretly showing his badge to him.

"You must inform your superior immediately. Have a look if you wish. Don't touch anything." He instructed.

"Of course, sir." He replied and they went inside the blast site.

Arjun saw the heavy rubble everywhere with broken tables and chairs. He looked at the granite topped counter cracked into pieces as well. They went upstairs to the terrace as well to see a blackish blast area in a corner. A few bits and pieces of rubber were seen.

Grenade up here. At least, one…

Arjun went back down and saw many blackened places like upstairs. They all checked around but Arjun noticed the intricate details around him.

Five…

He looked at another few.

Must be seven… seven bombs on this floor? And what are they?
Maybe dynamite…with a timer for sure.

"Hey, kid!" called out the head officer.

"Yes, sir?" replied Arjun.

"Tell your superior that there was one blast on the terrace
in the exact same place where her student Rishi Aggarwal
died. Anything you found?" he asked.

"I'm in high school. What can I get?" said Arjun, sarcastically.
The officers chuckled.

"Okay, well one blast up. A bomb of rubber. Five to six blasts
down here. Maybe normal dynamite. Okay?" he said.

"Yes, sir." Arjun replied and left.

After duty, Gaurav, Radhika and Simran discuss in the
meeting room. Simran checks out the passports.

"I can identify this girl but the other guy is a mystery. This girl is on that list of Prakash's accomplices." – opening her laptop and typing – "Here. This is her, right?" asked Simran, showing the laptop on which had a picture.

"Yes! That's it! Who is she?" asked Gaurav.

"Niharika Rai. Natasha's sister. I don't think she's in contact with her." Said Radhika.

"Is she here for another deal?" asked Gaurav.

"I don't know. But go inform Princi and we're calling the Director now. She spells trouble." Said Radhika.

Gaurav nodded and left. They connect to the Director and tell her everything.

"Hmm…I see." She said.

"What to do now?" asked Simran.

"I'm going to run an enquiry on her. I'm also going to investigate the various possibilities of Prakash's hide out. The shipment was coming from a remote area in Pakistan. Some agents are enquiring. Also,I'll put a search for that man on the other passport. Okay?" said the Director.

"Till then?" asked Radhika.

"Inform our defence sector for rounds." She said.

Elsewhere, in a hotel conference hall in the heart of Madrid, Spain had Lu, Prakash and Brad with another man called Dean, one of Prakash's right-hand men and advisors. He is very good with technology. A few well-built men stood guard at the door inside and outside. A couple were at the window.

"How can you just return with nothing?" scolded Brad.

"You've failed at what I've asked you to do! We are very low on our budget. We still haven't met half of our expenses for our upcoming project! It took forever to get that dealer! What do you plan on doing now?!" asked Dean, very annoyed.

"I had an entire battalion of police in the area where I was! They knew everything! I don't even know how!" said Lu. "Young and agile officers were there! I was surprised that they could take me on!"

"That's very rare coming from you! The shipment must be with them as well! Which address is written on it?" asked Dean.

"Some area near Lahore, Pakistan." Said Lu.

"Good." Said Dean.

"How?" asked Lu.

"That centre is shifted to Kabul now. Taliban is providing security." Said Dean.

"Shift it to the project area. Kabul is not safe. American soldiers are there." Said Prakash, finally speaking.

"Wait! What project area?!" asked Brad.

They fell silent.

"You stay with Dean at the project facility. Brad, you too. Our other partner is now on a quest and another one is helping her." Said Prakash.

"It's still risky. Do you really think it's in that LOCKER?" asked Dean.

"It has to be. I know that it was put there. And it hasn't been opened since." Said Prakash. "Just wait."

"But her sister is there. She's a top 50 agent. You know how deadly they are." Said Dean.

"I don't know who, but some of my guys got hurt badly by one of them. We were at LOCKER 01." Said Brad.

"That's exactly where she is going to." Said Dean.

"Show that girl's picture." Said Lu.

Dean typed a little in his laptop and frowned.

"I'm not able to hack in. It's too protected." Said Dean.

"What did you expect, then? Just let her go do her job. I've already taken care of the most intelligent one. And another one who knew too much." Said Prakash.

"Can you get anybody's picture from there?" asked Lu.

Dean typed a little and showed one picture of a hefty girl. It was marked 'Deceased'.

"We got her killed. Her parents are known to you." Said Prakash.

"Anybody else?" asked Lu.

"The other one's photo is inaccessible. She was a hacker. So, she kept herself hidden from the internet. By the way, can you identify anybody significant of that police force that almost caught you?" asked Dean.

"All of them were so young. I've never seen anybody perfectly." She said.

"Then leave it. We'll ask her when she gets back." Said Prakash.

Lu and Dean left after a couple of minutes.

"She was supposed to get the money and the shipment? This chick is ruining our trust with our customers!" said Brad.

"I can't help it. It was important for the project area." Said Prakash.

"What project area?!" asked Brad, frustrated.

"When you go there, you will get to know. Trust me." Said Prakash.

"Why did you let that Rai go, anyway?" asked Brad.

"She was given orders from the boss." Replied Prakash.

"You knew before, ma'am?" asked Gaurav, surprised.

He was standing in front of the Principal alone in her cabin while she was sitting with a file in her hand.

"Arjun already found information from the police. Didn't he tell you this?" asked the Principal.

But how was he there?! How could he-I have to ask him!

"I didn't know he would come and tell you. No problem then." Said Gaurav, covering up.

"Okay. Well, Prakash wanted Rishi gone too so…" she said.

"He got Rishi killed too?" exclaimed Gaurav.

"Most likely. Other top 400 agents were murdered with the same arsenal." She said.

He was dumbfounded at his theory proven right!

"Mind going back to work now?" she asked.

"Sorry! Sorry, ma'am. I'm leaving." He said and rushed out of the cabin.

On his way to the hostels, he called up Radhika and Simran on Radhika's phone and told them everything.

"So, Prakash got Rishi killed?" said Radhika.

"Yeah, and this Arjun came after we left the scene of the blast. I'm going to kill him. He always hides stuff! I'm going to find out what he knows right now!" said Gaurav in anger while walking up the hostel stairs.

"No! Don't do it!" said Radhika.

Gaurav stopped.

"Why? I should find out! He knows exactly what happened! He's a bomb expert!" said Gaurav.

"Listen to me, Gaurav! If you ask him, he'll know that we know about the blast as well as he does. He might think that we know more. Do not say a word to him. Act normal or else he'll come onto us. Understand?!" Simran instructed.

"Okay…" he replied and left towards his room.

A couple of days later, Radhika and Simran went to the police station. Radhika got down and went inside. One constable stands and greets her which she returns. He reached into his pocket and handed her a crumpled paper. She nodded and left. She went out, gave it to Simran and they went back to school.

At night duty, Simran reached the surveillance room to find it locked.

Where is this guy?!

She goes to the hostels and climbs up the stairs to the topmost floor. She walks till the end and finds Arjun's room door slightly open. She peeked inside to see Arjun and Gaurav there. They were in the middle of a conversation. Neerav was there too but wasn't directly involved.

"What were you doing in town during the blast?" said Gaurav.

"I was in town at a doctor's clinic. I wanted to check my burns. It was pure coincident that the blast happened." Arjun replied.

"You said you didn't need checking." Said Gaurav.

"What are you trying to say here?" asked Arjun.

"Hey, come on! Arjun, calm down. He's not accusing you of it!" said Neerav, interjecting.

"I'm not crazy. Wait a bit, Neerav. You didn't bother to tell anybody about the blast when you came back?" said Gaurav, getting angry.

"I told the Principal! What are you getting at here?" asked Arjun.

"Gaurav, hey! Arjun, Calm down- "started Neerav.

"Don't interrupt me!" said Gaurav, sternly.

"What do you want anyway? "asked Arjun.

"Obviously I want to know what happened! It was a blast and you know a lot about bombs, right?" said Gaurav.

"You think I'm that good to examine the place and not tell everything I know- "started Arjun.

"Obviously! You always do a lot of things like that and we can't solve anything! Don't you want to help the Director- "Gaurav started.

"Arh! I don't give a damn! And anyway, Simran, Radhika and you always have something going on and none of us know about it!" said Arjun.

"You wouldn't help us even if we told you! We three may not trust each other but we are damn sure on doubting you!" said Gaurav.

"So it's not just me?!" exclaimed Neerav.

"What do you mean?" asked Gaurav, puzzled.

"You also doubt him going out so late mysteriously, right?" said Neerav.

That wasn't Ajay?! It was him! But why?!

"Uh…yeah! Which brings us back to what were you doing in town?" said Gaurav.

"Stop it!!" shouted Arjun, getting annoyed.

"I'm interested in knowing too!" said Neerav.

"You get lost, Neerav! And you, snitch-for-those-two-girls, leave me alone or else-" Said Arjun.

"Or else what? "asked Gaurav, taunting him.

"I'll get Nikhil to handle you!" said Arjun.

"As if I'm scared of him!" – walking towards the door but turning around – "I'm onto you, Arjun!" said Gaurav and left outside.

Simran was sticking to the ceiling with her stick gloves. Gaurav was walking when suddenly he stopped and looked up at her. They had an eye contact. Gaurav did not say a word and left. Simran left as well to the surveillance room and unlocked it herself.

Later, at dinner, Gaurav pulled Simran to a table alone and sat her down.

"I can't believe you did that! Arjun now knows we are onto something!" she said.

"If I was that good with sticking to the ceiling, I would have not done this. You eavesdropped on everything, didn't you?" he said.

"You all were late for duty. I came to call Arjun. I didn't expect to hear this. Then again, I'm glad I did." She said.

"I would've done the same. He's too suspicious now. I was noticing a guy leaving out the gate after bedtime at least two nights a week. It would either be Ajay or an agent. Neerav cleared that up now." He said.

Simran brooded silently for a while.

"Don't think about this, okay? We are not trusting him." Said Gaurav.

"I know, I know!" she said.

But he trusts me in a few things. What can I do?

Chapter Nine – LOCKER robbed?!

"No freaking way!" exclaimed Radhika at hearing from Simran about the argument of the three boys yesterday.

They were in the study hall at break time.

"I'm not kidding." Said Simran.

"It's personal, I guess…does Arjun really hate you that much?" asked Radhika.

"I don't know. I don't even care but he has some information that we don't know. That's for sure." Said Simran.

"Don't you think Nikhil would know?" asked Radhika.

"Nikhil isn't even hanging around with him nowadays."
She said.

"How do you know that?" she asked.

"He's always around us-I mean, around me. But anyway,
I doubt a lot of things. He's not completely faithful to the
LSS." She said.

"Hey, don't say that! I thought you said he left all his business
behind. He told you that." She said.

"Yeah, he did…" said Simran.

But that was when he kept lying to me all the time.

Later, at a few places in the school, Simran noticed a few
guys fixing the cameras. She reached the surveillance room.

"Did you call for them? The ones who are fixing the
cameras?" asked Simran.

"Yeah, why?" he asked.

"You didn't have to. It was only a signal problem because of
the rain." She said.

"What's the big deal?" he asked.

"It's not like that. We just have a budget." She said.

"It'll be useful, trust me." He said.

"Yeah right." She said.

Tomorrow, during break time, in the Study hall, Simran and Radhika talk.

"To fix the cameras? We are already low on money. And don't the cameras have signal problems because of the weather?" Said Radhika.

"You know; it's been quite sunny for the past few days. Why would the cameras stop working then?" asked Simran.

"I don't know, but we still have other things to worry about." Said Radhika.

"Yeah…" said Simran.

They continued studying.

At night duty, in the Surveillance room,

"Arjun, are you sure the cameras were not working?" asked Simran.

"Of course!" he said.

"Are you absolutely sure?" she asked.

"Jeez! Are you that worried about our budget?!" he asked.

"No, it's not that." She said.

"Then what is it?!" he asked.

"Nothing!" she said.

"You'll never tell me anyway! So annoying!" he said.

"Hey, what's that supposed to mean?" she asked.

"Come on! What is it going to take you to tell me?!" he asked.

"I just won't!" she said, looking at the monitors.

"Tell me! Simran!" he said.

"Don't disturb me!" she said.

"How did you save me?! It's a simple question!" he said.

She didn't answer.

"You are impossible! You don't say anything about yourself, your family, your test scores- "he started.

"Again, with the test scores! What is your problem?! I don't like you, I don't trust you, I don't want you to know about me and whatever I did, I did it to save you because we're partners. That's all you need to know!" she said, annoyed.

"Arh! I give up!" he said angrily and left the room.

Just then, the LOCKER alarm was set off in the surveillance room! Simran noticed the camera in the basement showing no signs of the LOCKER being opened but noticed a guard roaming back and forth, getting cut off! The tape was looped in the camera! Simran checked a few other cameras and finally caught Niharika on the screens with a bag pack! Simran immediately ran out. She saw Arjun walking away in the same direction. She quickly grabs his hand and drags him with her while running!

"What the hell- "he started.

"She's getting away! We have to go after her! We're closest to the bikes and exits! Come on!" Simran exclaimed.

"Who?!" he exclaimed.

Arjun immediately calls up Nikhil and tells him! Nikhil and everybody else go down to the LOCKER basement! The Principal also reached and they were all shocked to see the huge metal door wide open!

"How the hell can this happen!?" exclaimed the Principal.

Arjun and Simran go outside to the parking to see Niharika getting away on a hover board! While Arjun saw her, Simran jumped on a bike and revved it up.

"Get on!" she called out.

Arjun quickly jumps on and they sped after her out the gate onto the Highway! As they gained on her,

"Hand me the bike! I'll drive!" shouted Arjun.

"Why?!" asked Simran.

"Start shooting her or else she'll get away!" he said.

"No! I can't!" she said.

"This is not the time to argue! Get up and start shooting!" he shouted.

She suddenly left the handles and he grabbed them.

"Come on! Get up!" he said.

"I'll fall!" she shouted.

"I got you! Get up!" he said.

"No!" she said.

"Trust me! I got you!" he said.

"Look who's talking!" she said.

He pulls her face towards his with one hand while controlling the bike with another and looks into her eyes.

"Trust me!" he said.

She gets up with her gun and aims but almost falls when Arjun wrapped his arm around her legs.

"Don't look down! Look at her!" he shouted.

She balanced herself and pointed her gun at the hover board. She then raised her aim higher at Niharika and shot a bullet successfully hitting her left shoulder. She yelped in pain and accidentally dropped her bag pack! She sped up more and so did they but suddenly a few rocks were seen on the road and Arjun saw at the last minute! He pressed the brakes and the bike skidded, making them fall off! Simran fell first with minor cuts but Arjun's legs and arms got a few burns because of the sparks created by the skidding bike! Niharika sped away and the bag pack was safe with Simran.

She immediately called an ambulance and rushed over to Arjun and pulled him away from the bike and held him carefully.

"Arjun! Arjun, hey! Can you hear me?!" she exclaimed, while wiping his face. "Are you okay?! Arjun!"

His eyes groggily looked at her.

"No..." he groaned in pain.

After an hour, Simran, Radhika, Gaurav, Nikhil and Aakash were looking through a window of a hospital room at Arjun. His left arm was in a cast and his burn marks were treated. He was sleeping.

"So, she got away..." said Nikhil.

"Don't start now, I don't want to deal with you." Said Simran.

Nikhil didn't say anything.

"Well, anything she took?" asked Aakash.

"Princi has the bag we recovered. But she has a file with her. An IB official will come tomorrow afternoon to seal the LOCKER again." Said Simran.

"The dilemma right now is that we need someone to spend a night in the basement near the LOCKER." Said Gaurav.

"I can stay the night." Said Radhika.

"I'll stay too." Said Simran.

"Good idea. Any problem, Nikhil?" asked Gaurav.

"Nope…let's go, then." He said and left with Aakash.

"I'll wait downstairs for you." Said Radhika and left with Gaurav.

Simran entered the room and sat next to Arjun laying down on the bed still sleeping. She slightly held his hand.

"You saved me…why did you do that and get hurt again?" she said.

A pause occurred.

"Last time, you told me to pretend to care about you…well, I do now…and it's real this time…" said Simran.

She went closer to him and felt his forehead. It was slightly warm. She pushed his hair back and slightly kissed his forehead.

"Thanks. I'll see you soon." She said and left.

Gaurav was outside. She nodded at him and left. She went back to school with Radhika and entered the basement with Radhika. Gaurav stayed at the hospital with Arjun.

In the LOCKER meeting room, Simran and Radhika entered. Radhika pulled the bag pack from under the table and emptied it. Out came a phone, a gun with ammo, a few bills, a few bundles of cash notes, a business card and a tiny phonebook. They both started looking at each of the things. Radhika picked up the phonebook and looked inside to find:

Shipment checking in from –

- *Moscow*

- *Chennai*

- *Lahore*

Verification address:

Radhika checked in all the pages for the missing information but it was empty. Simran checked the phone and the gun. Radhika then looked at the bills and the business card:

Kapoor Enterprise #221-3346

Shipments are at a cost but products are worth all the trouble.

She flipped the card and something was written.

You are going to die…

"Simran…" she said, while showing the card.

"Was she here for business as well?" asked Simran, confused.

"I don't know, maybe she was going to give this as a threat. It would've been blank otherwise." She said.

Simran held up the cell phone.

"You know how to hack that?" asked Radhika.

"It's a long process. This phone is special." She said. "But I can do it."

"Okay, then. What else?" asked Radhika.

"Nothing else, I guess. Let's hope this is sealed quickly." Said Simran.

"We'll tell the Director tomorrow." Said Radhika.

Chapter Ten – The truth...

In the morning, Simran and Radhika were in the LOCKER corridor sleeping next to each other. Suddenly they woke up with the sound of the basement door opening. Gaurav came in, while yawning.

"Weren't you at the hospital?" asked Simran, getting up while yawning.

"Yeah, we just came back. He's resting in his room." He said.

"Okay, good." Said Radhika, giving her hand out.

Simran yawned just then. Gaurav then grabbed her hand and pulled her up.

"Thank you…" she said.

"I've got bad news, though." He said.

"What?"

"The LOCKER has to stay open for a while longer." He said.

"What?! Why?!" exclaimed Radhika.

"Niharika stole a file and we have to get that back. It's really important to seal it away." Said Gaurav.

"So how long is this going to be open?" asked Simran.

"A week? A month? A few months? Who knows." Said Gaurav.

"Damn!" said Radhika, with her hand on her forehead.

"The good news is that we have a few defence personnel from ma'am's sector to patrol the LOCKER area." Said Gaurav.

"Okay."

"By the way…just for confidentiality," – bending his head low and the other two following – "Did you find anything useful in that back pack?" he asked.

"Nothing interesting except a cell phone. But it will take time to hack." Said Radhika.

"How come? It's just a cell phone." He said.

"It's secured tight. It has a lot of walls and once we are through them, in a couple weeks, tops, there is a passkey with only three guesses. If guessed wrong…" Simran shook her head with a frown.

"Then what?" asked Gaurav.

"It'll blast." Said Radhika.

They went to meeting room and connected to the Director informing her of everything.

"Well, I can't make out anything of the given information. But if you are sure that you can get into that phone, then try your luck. Okay?" said the Director.

"Yes, ma'am." They said.

She cut the call after a few minutes.

In an hour, the Director was called to the Board Member N. Manisha's cabin. She went in and sat down.

"I'm really sorry for what happened." Said the Director.

"Sorry? How could you? I thought you wouldn't let this happen!" she said.

"Nobody saw it coming. It was too swift for anyone to notice. I had close eyes on LOCKER 01." She said.

"So Niharika Rai did it. I guess, it's safe to say that Prakash is not leaving us alone. But we have half the force looking for him! I can't do anything else!" she said.

"The LSS top 400 at LOCKER 01 are well connected with me, all of them are. The agents said they will give some information from a few things they acquired." She said.

"Don't involve children-" She started.

"The agency might be infiltrated. I have no choice." She said.

Manisha sighed and leaned into her chair.

"Am I supposed to be worried that he has a personal vendetta with you? And maybe your top 400 at LOCKER 01 because they all had a part to play in his arrest!" she said.

"What are you trying to say?" she asked.

"A robbery attempt first, two agents from that squad dead, a blast at the crime scene of the second dead agent and now a successful robbery! I want this nightmare to end!" she said.

"And I'm trying my best to do that." She replied.

"I want this as priority one for you. I will keep check on your progress myself. Maybe we can end this together." she said.

"Yeah, maybe." Replied the Director.

After school hours, Simran went to the boys' side of the hostels and went upstairs to the top floor with a file in her hands. She reached and walked straight to the last room. She knocked on the door. After a few seconds, Neerav opened it.

"Hey, what's up?" he greeted.

"Hey!" – coming inside and noticing Arjun not there – "Where did he go?" she asked.

"He went to wash his face. What's in there?" he asked, pointing at the file.

"Oh, yeah!" – opening it and taking out a picture to show him – "Do you know this guy?" she asked.

"Hmm…" – seeing the photograph carefully – "No, sorry. Why?" he asked.

"He was seen around here…it's okay, I'm asking everybody." Said Simran.

Just then, Neerav gets a call and he goes to open the door when Arjun comes in. Neerav left outside to talk and Arjun entered slowly while taking support of the wall. He stopped at seeing her. They looked at each other for a moment when Arjun broke their eye contact.

"Could you help me till my bed?" he asked.

She put the file on his bed and goes to him. His right hand was on the wall and the other was holding his right waist. She puts her right arm at the waist and his left arm around her shoulder then helps him till his bed. He reaches and sits down, while letting go of her.

"You don't look okay. You should've stayed in the hospital for a while longer." Said Simran.

"Is that concern, I hear?" he asked.

She didn't reply and thought.

It might be…

"I guess I owe you a couple of explanations." She said, standing in front of him.

"I swear to god, now you owe me an explanation for every damn thing or else I'll keep getting injured like this, protecting you for no reason I find valid and risking our lives and jobs! Got it?" He said, getting fed up.

Simran closed the door and bolted it. She closed the curtains as well.

"Okay, ask me. I'll tell you everything." She said.

"How'd you figure it was Niharika Rai?" he asked.

"At the blasted coffee shop, Gaurav found her passport. I knew her association with Prakash. I should have expected something like this." She said.

A pause occurred.

"You shot the guy dead, right? When Aparna died?" he asked.

"Yes." She said, sitting down on a chair.

"When Brad came, you killed at least three of his men, right? Was that you?" he asked.

"I didn't kill them…I just injured them badly…with a knife…" she said.

He chuckled. She looked at him in confusion.

"You shoot good. Why shouldn't anyone know?" he asked.

"I rarely shoot. So, no need to tell." she said.

"Why?" he asked.

"It brings bad memories…" she said.

"Wow…" he said.

"What's so 'wow' in that?" she asked.

"Something in common." – nudging her slightly – "Fainting brings bad memories to me." He said.

"No, that's you and Indu. Ask her." She said.

He was surprised.

"Anything else?" she asked.

"Last one, where are you in your little investigation?" he asked.

She showed the picture she showed Neerav before.

"You know this guy?" she asked. "I'm stuck with him. He was seen here with Niharika."

"I never saw this guy." He said, after a good look.

"It's okay…" she said.

There was a pause.

"Were you at the hospital with me yesterday night? I swear, I think I saw you in my room." He said.

"I was with you while you were awake. After you slept, I went back. I kept guard in the basement all night." She said.

"We all should take turns, huh. To see that thing." He said.

"Yeah…" she said.

There was another pause.

"Well, I should get some sleep." He said.

"Yeah…" – getting up and taking her file – "Thanks, by the way." She said.

"For what?" he asked.

"For saving my life." She said.

"Likewise, Miss know it all." He said, giving a small smile.

She turned and left out the door.

She did kiss me; I swear she did…

He thought.

Simran went out and shut the door after her. She walked with her file back to her room. She entered, closed the door and sat down on her bed looking at the photo again.

I did see this guy before. But his photo is erased. Nothing is there. How am I going to find this guy?

She sighed and kept the file in her desk drawer. She opened another drawer to check her laptop with the cell phone plugged in it. She lifted the phone to see a message written saying "Forgot your password? Three attempts only." She opened her laptop and it immediately showed a screen showing a dialog box saying "Software ready." She then typed something and connected the phone again. She continued to work.

Meanwhile, in the basement, the Principal, Gaurav and Indira were standing behind Radhika in front of the LOCKER door while she was typing in her laptop. It was connected to a circuit board in front of the door. A couple of officers from the defence sector were also standing there. Radhika pushed her glasses up and continued typing in her laptop. After a few minutes, the space between the main door and the other was filled with red lines from every direction. She continued typing a little more. After a couple of minutes, she closed her laptop and beckoned Gaurav to come. He looked at the rest looking at him then went to her. "Unplug these wires from the board." She said and he did so. She handed her laptop to him. He held onto it while she fixed back a slab firmly. She then took back her laptop while he held onto the wires. They turned around.

"Alarm triggered lasers are enabled. It can help us for the time being. You can only disable it manually by standing here. It's all I can do." Said Radhika.

"It's more than enough, Agent Chopra. But Agent Jaiswal?" called out the Principal.

"Yes, ma'am?" she asked.

"Put two people here every night. It's still not safe." Said the Principal.

"Understood." She said.

The Principal left.

"How about you two stay here tonight? Just to check the alarm system?" asked Indira.

"Yeah, surely." Said Radhika, looking at Gaurav.

"Yeah, I'm fine." He said, looking at Radhika.

Back at the hostels, Simran finished enabling a software making the screen of the mobile blurred. She kept her laptop back in her drawer with the phone then lied down on her bed in thought.

If nothing useful comes from that phone, then we'll hit a dead end. I'll just have to wait…

She continued to think for some time.

Arjun really got hurt this time…worse than before…I shouldn't have kissed him…at least, he was sleeping…Simran, what is wrong with you? Don't start being so close to him! It's nothing… let's just hope he gets better.

Arjun did not sleep. He spent time thinking while looking at his sim card. His phone was crushed but his sim card was saved.

Why can't I sleep? And my sim card wasn't crushed…it should have…no! What am I saying? How will I continue my deals? But this bad habit could've gone by the smash of a card… should I do it?

He continued thinking.

Chapter Eleven – Memories.

In the basement, near the LOCKER, Radhika and Gaurav sat in front of the open main door watching the lasers still on.

"Arjun's injuries?" asked Radhika.

"He'll be fine in another week. He was supposed to stay at the hospital but he was in a hurry to come back." Replied Gaurav.

"How come?"

"He wanted to see Simran. She won't tell him everything, right?"

"Of course, she won't."

"Good...let's hope we get something out of the phone."

"I think an address will come."

"You're hoping for an address?" he asked, looking at her.

She nodded.

"It wouldn't matter. Their hideout keeps changing. If we go look for it, then they will just escape. It will be a waste of time for us." He said.

"Wait, you coming?" she asked.

"What's the problem in it? I'm not letting you guys go without me!"

"We'll be fine; you don't need to come."

"I know but I want to get the bad guys with you. I'm too bored with my life. Who knows if we get another mission or not?"

"Okay...good. So, that's your reason."

"Oh, you'll be fine without anybody. But I want to have fun. And with you..."

Elsewhere, in New Delhi, the entire LSS Headquarters were dark now of night. Only one small lamp was on in the

Director's cabin as she was working late. She had trouble concentrating due to her lack of sleep from the past few days. Her eyes kept on drooping down as she was reading a file. After half an hour, she was fast asleep in her chair...

Twenty-two years ago,

"Hey! Agent Kapoor!" called out Vijayanti, stopping a young man in the corridor of the LSS branch of the IB in Mumbai. He turned around with an unpleasant face but gave a smile. "Yes, Agent Rao?" he replied.

"The Head is calling us and...wait, where's Agent Khanna?" she asked.

"I don't know. Maybe he slept late again or something- "he started.

"I'm here! I've reached! I'm in time!" shouted Agent Khanna from the other side of the corridor while running over to them wearing a back pack on one shoulder.

He stopped in front of them, bent down and gave one breath of exhaustion. He then immediately stood properly looking as energetic as ever.

"You're not on time, though. I really wonder when you would grow up." She said.

"All right, Vijayanti. Get to the point." Said Prakash.

"I really don't know the details but dad's calling us now." She said.

They left to the top floor and were standing in front of the Head in his office. He was smoking while looking in a file. After a few silent minutes passed by, he closed the file and put it on his desk. He then pushed it forward for them to take.

"This person is to be arrested at all costs. He robbed LOCKER 02. All of it. He plans on selling every file in it. He is headed for another too. You must find out and catch him. You also need to seal LOCKER 02 after investigation. Understood?" he said.

"Yes, sir!"

"You leave after two hours. Here are your tickets." He said and placed them on the file.

Agent Rao took it and the three of them left outside. In the corridor,

"Well! He didn't leave a paper behind. He definitely had people with him." Said Agent Kapoor, looking in the file.

"I suspect the top 400." Said Agent Khanna.

"How come? And what help would they be in opening the LOCKER?" asked Agent Rao.

"Well, I saw the graduates of this year. They are not impressive. Majority were in juvenile." Said Agent Kapoor.

"What the hell were those officials thinking?" Agent Rao exclaimed.

"No idea, but I'm getting a feeling that we'll need a few more people with us when we go." Said Agent Khanna.

"Good idea." Said Agent Rao.

They spent the next one hour grabbing a few others as they can. In the main Surveillance room of the building, Agent Khanna went inside and went to a young lady sitting on a chair in front of the cameras with a Bluetooth in her ear talking. She had very similar features to that of Simran.

"Hey! Agent Akhtar!" – she did not respond – "Agent Akhtar!" – still not responding - "Naazira!" he said out loud.

Everyone stopped and turned to their direction. So did Agent Akhtar.

"I'll get back to you!" she said and turned off the Bluetooth. She gave one look of death to the people looking at them and they immediately turned back to their work.

"What do you want, Agent Khanna?" she asked.

"We're going on a mission and we leave in another hour. Come with us!" he said.

"I can't leave here. The Head will kill me!" she said.

"Great, why did I even ask?" he said.

"What's that supposed to mean?" she asked, folding her arms.

"You never say yes to anything! Whenever I come offering to take you to a mission, a dinner, a movie, anything! You say no!" he said.

"That's not true! We've went out!" she said.

"Oh really! When?" he asked.

A pause came. Everybody was edging their ears closer to them.

"Right now!" she said, grabbing her bag pack and putting her Bluetooth down.

"Wait, seriously?" he asked.

"Yeah, what the heck!" she said and got up.

She leaves then looks back at the others.

"We got you covered!" said one.

"Just go!" said another.

Meanwhile, Agent Kapoor and Agent Rao go to the Technical room where there were a lot of computers.

"You seriously want to get them?" asked Agent Kapoor.

"Trust me, they'll seal the LOCKER in no time." Said Agent Rao.

They looked around for a while and spot a lanky young man in the thickest of all glasses and went over to him.

"Zain! Hey, you busy?" asked Agent Rao.

"Not much, why?" he asked.

"We need to investigate and seal a LOCKER quickly. Can you come?" asked Agent Kapoor.

"When are you leaving?" he asked.

"An hour." Said Agent Rao.

"My file and laptop are in my apartment. We'll have to go get it." He said.

"Well, then we've got no time to waste! Let's go!" said Agent Rao, leaving with Agent Kapoor dragging Zain with them.

After landing in Bhopal, the five of them enter in a car waiting for them and leave on the national highway. They take a few hours to reach a small town and a school. There were a few army commandos standing there talking when they saw them. They all get down and go to the gate where they were stopped.

"ID?" asked one army official.

All five of them show their LSS badges all together. The badges of LSS officials were exactly like the ones of the top 400 but without the numbers noted down.

"Go! Someone escort them!" said the official.

The gate opened and they all rushed inside with two commandos in front of them. They noticed the entire school empty due to the summer holidays. They reached the stairway and went downstairs to the basement where there was their undercover LSS Agent or Principal of the school standing in front of it with a few commandos.

Agent Rao went and shook hands with the Principal. He felt puzzled.

"IB Mumbai, LSS Branch! I'm Agent Rao." She greeted.

"Oh! Agent Rao, very well! I'll leave you to it!" he said, handing her a file and leaving with a commando.

She looked through it briefly and handed it over to Agent Kapoor. He took it and looked through it in detail.

"Agent Khanna, Zain and Agent Akhtar. Let's check it out inside." Said Agent Rao and they all went inside the empty LOCKER room with Agent Kapoor coming in after them still looking in the file.

They started wearing their gloves on and started investigating. After a couple of hours, they all came out. They then went outside to see all the LSS Agents assigned to LOCKER 02 standing outside with the Principal. They stood in front of them. Agent Rao took a step forward.

"Good Morning, top 400. First, the investigation of LOCKER 02 is now transferred formally to us. Secondly, we are not authorised to tell you anything about ourselves. Just know that we are from the Intelligence regarding these matters. It's our regular job. Lastly, we hold no suspicions on you because you work for us and the LOCKER's safety but still we expect some cooperation while we enquire from each of you on what happened that night. Understood?" said Agent Rao.

"Yes, ma'am!" they all replied.

"All right, girls can go to my left and boys on my right. Follow them to a comfortable place for questioning. Now!" said Agent Rao.

The girls went to Agent Akhtar and the boys to Agent Khanna. They left with them and a few commandos. Agent Rao, Agent Kapoor, Zain and the Principal left to the meeting room next to the LOCKER and sat down to discuss their findings.

"Well!" – thumping the file on the table – "This file is useless now. There is nothing in here!" said Agent Kapoor.

"There are bundles of papers in there." Said Zain.

"It's all on things we know about him. But it will never be enough on how to find this guy. He's like a ghost." Said Agent Kapoor.

"Anything from the LOCKER?" asked the Principal.

"We've found a few things. A few papers, a few bullets, etc. But one thing is very unusual which I found." Said Agent Rao.

"What?" they all asked.

She held out a small, metallic pin looped at one end and placed it on the table. Agent Kapoor and Zain were surprised. The Principal was shocked.

"How the hell is that there?" asked the Principal.

"I don't know, I just found it in the LOCKER." Said Agent Rao.

"But the LOCKER wasn't having any blast marks anywhere!" said the Principal.

"Most likely it's the only explanation that one of the robbers took out the pin in the LOCKER but then went outside and threw the grenade…and we can understand from this that if you have to physically throw a grenade, it won't land so far. The blast might've definitely been heard by someone in the evening." Deduced Agent Kapoor.

"So we have to wait for some answers from the top 400." Said Agent Rao.

There was a silence. Everyone in the room were waiting patiently.

After a few minutes, Agent Khanna entered. Everyone looked at him optimistically but he frowned and shook his head. He went and sat down with them and they all continued to stay silent.

Suddenly, Agent Akhtar rushed inside the room still having her gun in her hand.

"You were right! The blast was heard by one agent! After some…uh…" – looking at her gun in her hand and tucking it in – "influence, she said that it was heard near the west side of the school. Let's go check it out!" she said.

They all immediately get up and leave. Agent Kapoor left the file in the room but Agent Rao took it and left after them. They run outside with a couple of commandos and went out of the gate. They go a few metres away from the compound wall to see the land scorched black! They put on their gloves and start looking around. The ground was scorched so much that even half of the trees and bushes were black too. Agent Khanna went to a bush and moved the branches to find something he felt. He pulled it out to see that it was a small sleek one shoulder bag pack. It was covered in black but some brown shades were also observed.

"OH MY GOD!" exclaimed Zain, suddenly.

Chapter Twelve – A connection?!

Zain was at another corner of the blast site where there were a few bushes and a couple trees blackened completely. He immediately stepped back and covered his nose at the terrible stench!

The rest of them went to where Zain checked and covered their noses as well. Agent Rao stood there still looking. Agent Akhtar and Agent Khanna stepped back and stood at a distance with Zain keeping their noses covered. Agent

Kapoor pulled the file from Agent Rao and looked in it again.

"You said it was useless!" said Zain, with his fingers pinching his nose close.

"Wait! I'm still checking!" he said.

"Agent Khanna, help me over here. Agent Akhtar, get some help. If you want to go too then you can, Zain! Make it quick!" said Agent Rao.

Agent Khanna went over.

"Help me move these." She said.

He broke a few branches of the bushes for a better visibility of what was there.

Later, they all were outside a mortuary waiting. After a few minutes, they were called inside.

"You guys go ahead." Said Zain.

"We can't take that smell." Said Agent Khanna.

"Please." Said Agent Akhtar.

Agent Rao and Agent Kapoor go inside the two-floored building. They pass by the reception and go for the stairs.

"Stop looking in the file, it's annoying." Said Agent Rao.

"I still think there's something…" – flipping through the pages – "I didn't see…" he replied.

"Prakash! Stop it! You know how annoying that is to me!" she said, standing in front of him.

He sighed and closed it.

"Happy now?" he asked.

"Yes!" she said and they continued walking.

In the room, there lay a body covered and a bag pack nearby.

"The grenade blasted in this fellow. So you can't properly identify his face. Nothing else found." Said the doctor leading the autopsy.

"So…he had that one grenade in him…but the blast radius was very big, a body can lessen that." Said Agent Kapoor.

"Someone definitely threw it outside. This guy was hit by accident." Said Agent Rao.

"So are they related? Or it was really an accident…" said Agent Kapoor.

"They are related. The defence protocols of the school don't allow any civilian to be anywhere within a few metres of the school, of course. This body must be one of the thieves." Said Agent Rao.

"Hmm…hey, is there a possibility for a fingerprint from the body?" asked Agent Kapoor.

The doctor checked to see one hand not there. It must've been blasted. The doctor then went around the table to check for the other hand. It was there and dirty.

"It's possible. I'll get a print for you. Please wait outside for a few minutes." He said.

They left outside and stood in the corridor waiting.

"A fingerprint can get us a lead, I guess." Said Agent Rao.

"Yeah…let's focus on other things. For one, we need to still hold onto that top 400 agent who admitted-wait! We need to hold onto all of them. They all know. There's no doubt." Said Agent Kapoor, looking down.

"Wait…first, you tell me what you know about them. Don't lie, I saw your reaction as soon as this guy's name was mentioned." – he looked up at her – "Start talking!" she said, pointing at him.

He sighed.

"It's them…the ones who I told you about." He said.

"You sure? They didn't show any attention since the last ten years." She said.

"Yeah, you're right. This is their first appearance since then." He said.

"I thought you said that they forgot about you." She said.

"Technically, they don't know where I am, who I am with, what I am doing now…they don't know anything about that…but…" he said.

"I thought you had dealt with those people. I still don't know what exactly did they do and you're not telling me." She said.

"I'm not telling you because there's no evidence. They did so much that they should just be taken out. They've done everything: robbing LOCKERs, killing our agents, hacking our defence networks and infiltrating" – pointing to himself – "the defence!" he said.

Agent Rao continued to listen.

"We are wasting our time whenever some LSS agent gets killed or some LOCKER is robbed. I've been waiting for this investigation to come under our charge for a long time." He said.

"It's come under Me, okay? Just don't do anything stupid. We are going to handle this properly and legally please." She said.

After a while, they got a fingerprint sample and went outside. Agent Khanna, Agent Akhtar and Zain were still waiting there.

"What happened?" asked Agent Khanna.

"The grenade was thrown on the body. Not sure if by accident. Face is not there. One arm and one limb missing. But a fingerprint was found. Zain!" – throwing a packet with a slide and him catching it – "Analyse that as fast as possible." Said Agent Rao.

"We need to re-interrogate the top 400 at the school. So let's go." Said Agent Kapoor.

"Okay alone, Zain?" asked Agent Rao.

"Yes, I'll have this scanned. I'll send a picture when I get it." Said Zain.

The rest left leaving Zain with a few commandos.

"This is an issued investigation. So you just start answering questions! Don't test my patience here!" Agent Rao said sternly.

"I swear! I just heard it at that place! The duty bell rang so I was going to sleep! That's when I heard it!" said the trembling agent.

They both were in a room darkened. A yellowish light emitting bulb hung from above and it flickered inconsistently.

"Then at least tell me this. You were not the only one to hear the blast. The others heard it too, didn't they?" said Agent Rao.

"Yes…they did…" she said, meekly.

"Lying to a detective here is an offense. I can suspend you from the LSS program." Said Agent Rao.

"Look, please don't! I can't afford a good school! I was told to not say anything by them! They said they keep watch on all of us! And if we slip up...please!" she said, scared.

"Tell me anything about them! Anything! Anything about the blast or the robbery! Anything!" said Agent Rao.

"I don't know much. They just planned to get another LOCKER. That's all. And I think they were fighting in the LOCKER. I heard shouts from them insulting each other." She said.

"How many were there?" she asked.

"Five, at least. Their faces were covered." She said.

"No civilian was nearby the school walls, right?" she said.

"It's protocol. The school is in the middle of nowhere and it's next to an army base. Nobody can just accidently slip in." she said.

"Okay..." said Agent Rao.

In the present, while everyone attended classes at school, Arjun was still thinking in his room with his sim card in his hand.

I'll have to do it…I…but I still can't…

After an hour, he goes down to the school with his hand bandaged and in a cast and sneaks into the basement. He goes to the meeting room and closed the door. He turned a few lights on and turned on the laptop. He clicked the link and it immediately connected to the Director.

"Arjun? You're not in class? What happened to your arm?" she asked.

"You didn't know?" he asked.

"I didn't expect it to be that serious. So you are here alone, huh." She said.

He didn't say anything.

"So, what do you want?" she asked.

"I'm sorry. I lied."

"About what?"

"Everything I was supposed to end."

"You still made deals with your bombs, didn't you? And Simran didn't keep an eye on you?"

"You put her there to watch me?"

"I did. I even told her but she didn't wish to be nosy. But why are you telling me this? I can inform your uncle if I wanted to."

"I just never owed anybody anything. Now I do. To pay that debt, I have to get rid of this."

"So, what's so hard about it?"

"I've been at this for four years…I don't want to regret it."

"I can give you a guarantee chance that you won't regret. Just do it." she said.

"Okay. Thank you, ma'am." He said.

"Rest well, Agent Singh." She said and went offline.

What happened to him, all of a sudden?

He turned off everything and left the room. He snuck out of the basement and walked till the stairs. He stopped in front of the LOCKER and gave a look at it. then he left out of the basement and snuck back to his hostel room. He took out the sim card and snapped it into two pieces.

Done…for good.

He threw the pieces and his old crushed phone in the trash.

"Zain! Did you get anything?" asked Agent Rao.

The others also reached the van where he was sitting in with his laptop still scanning the fingerprint sample. The laptop was next to him while he sat and looked around bored.

"Well, look at your surroundings. This is called nature." Said Agent Khanna.

"Ugh…I was so bored. Fingerprint scans take so much time, especially when we're not in the main building. What did you guys get?" asked Zain.

"The thieves were fighting in the LOCKER. So our theory is right. That body is one of theirs." Said Agent Rao.

Suddenly there was a loud beeping sound coming from the laptop. Everybody turned to the sound and Zain immediately picked it up and started typing again. After a few minutes of doing so, he pressed enter and a picture started loading slowly.

"All right. Know him?" asked Zain, turning the laptop around.

"Oh shit!" they all said.

Agent Akhtar covered her mouth. Agent Khanna folded his hands and shook his head. Agent Rao's hand was pressing her forehead. Agent Kapoor just froze with wide open eyes still looking at the picture.

"Guys…who is he?" asked Zain, very confused.

"He's a recruit of LeT. What's he doing with them?" asked Agent Khanna.

"Zain, what all types of documents are kept in LOCKER 02? Just check." Said Agent Rao.

He looked into his laptop and started typing again for some time.

"Wait, different LOCKERs have one type of files in them?" asked Agent Akhtar.

"Yes, the LOCKERs are different categories. Rarely some are opened but it helps to be better organized." Said Agent Rao.

"LOCKER 02 consists of government building plans. Any government building plan before 1984 was in that LOCKER." Said Zain.

"Oh shit." Said Agent Rao.

"Well, what to do?" asked Zain.

They all thought for a while.

"Send that photo to all LSS branches. Tell them to spread that photo to every city and town police near their respective LOCKERs. Now." Said Agent Rao.

Zain started typing in his laptop.

"Agent Khanna, print a few copies of that picture and hand it to all of us. In another hour, we'll go around the neighbouring villages and towns and ask as many people about this guy." Said Agent Rao.

He nodded and left.

"Any picture on the guy in that file, Agent Kapoor?" asked Agent Rao when she saw him again looking in the file.

"Umm…" he searched.

"Agent Akhtar, tell security to send more defence personnel for a few days. That school will be under lockdown until we get the files back. Now." Said Agent Rao.

She immediately left. Agent Rao sat down next to Zain and pressed her forehead. After a few minutes, Agent Kapoor went to her and gave a bottle of water. He put the file in her hands.

"I got a photo. I'll print this out too." He said and left.

She took a few gulps of water down and kept the bottle aside. Zain finished typing and put his laptop down.

"Done!" he said.

"Now we wait…" she replied.

Chapter Thirteen – A crucial decision.

After an hour, everybody went out to the nearby two villages and two towns. They went to each major area and showed the two photos asking anything about them. This took most of their time during the day, just going everywhere and showing photos, asking their whereabouts and finding nothing useful. After a couple of hours, the team met back near the gate of the school campus of LOCKER 02.

"Anybody found anything? I didn't." said Agent Rao.

"Neither did I." said Agent Khanna, folding his arms.

"Same here." Said Agent Akhtar, frowning.

"No clue, huh." Said Zain.

"Agent Kapoor…he's not back yet." Said Agent Rao, looking in the road's direction.

"These people are like ghosts." Said Agent Akhtar.

"How are we supposed to find them?" wondered Agent Khanna.

Just then, Prakash and his team arrived in their jeep. He got down and went over to them still holding the file in his hands.

"Sorry, I'm late. I found out about a rental car used by them to escape. They directly went to an airstrip. I don't know where they went from there but that airstrip is used by defence. Sometimes missile testing is done there. They might have known someone to get away." Said Agent Kapoor.

"Wow…they really are ghosts." Said Agent Akhtar.

They all continued discussing.

"I need to speak to you alone." Agent Kapoor whispered to Agent Rao.

"Okay…" she replied.

He found out something else, didn't he?

Later on, everybody went to their hotel in the town nearby the school, checked into their individual rooms and slept while Agent Rao and Agent Kapoor were in one room discussing. Only one lamp was on.

"So what happened?" asked Agent Rao.

"Don't worry, the airstrip is there and I didn't lie about that. But I think that I was followed from the airstrip." Said Agent Kapoor.

"Why did you check us in this hotel, then?" she asked.

"One or half a kilometre away is the army base. I have their numbers too so we're sorted." He said.

"So…those guys might contact you? Or kill you?" she asked.

"They contacted me." – handing his phone to show a number – "Trace it." He said.

Just then, the room door opened to reveal Agent Khanna. He closed it after him.

"Give it to me. I'll do it myself." Said Agent Khanna.

Agent Kapoor handed over his phone to him.

"Why were you eavesdropping?" asked Agent Rao.

"Well, I had a hunch that you two were planning something crazy. Are you?" asked Agent Khanna.

"No, no, no! Nothing crazy is going to happen!" said Agent Rao.

"Oh come on!" he said.

"Just trace that number and we'll see." Said Agent Kapoor.

"Okay, fine!" said Agent Khanna and left.

"I've traced it to Bengaluru. Here." – printing out an address and their tickets – "We'll leave in three hours." Said Agent Khanna.

It was the next morning and everybody was there having breakfast in a café together. Zain then arrived.

"I've temporarily sealed the LOCKER." He said.

"Good job." Said Agent Rao.

In the plane to Bengaluru,

"Prakash, don't do anything reckless. We'll calmly plan this." Said Agent Rao.

"They know everything. They are trying to convince me to help them cross the border. They know where I work and whom all I work with." He said.

"We're all doing this together. Don't believe their bluffs and try to fix things by yourself. More than them, we need the stuff of the LOCKER. And we should try our best to get them alive. No killing until we find the stuff." She said.

"Okay…" he said.

After they reached, they went and met with a few officers who gave them pictures of the area and a map. They went to the area and asked around showing the pictures of the two men. One shopkeeper pointed in a diagonal direction across the main road to a small PCO box saying that the person was talking to someone from there in the afternoon yesterday. After this, the team went to an old warehouse and planned.

"Most likely, we can find-"

Agent Rao was interrupted by phone ringing. Everybody checked their phones. The phone ring was Agent Kapoor's.

He took it out and was wide eyed at seeing the number. It was them.

"Zain, trace it." Said Agent Rao.

They all put on headphones. Agent Rao checked everyone them signalled Agent Kapoor to answer the call.

"Hello?" answered Agent Kapoor.

"Well, you know me. We spoke on the phone before. You know what I do. I gave you time to decide." Said a deep voice on the other line.

"Yes, you did. Well, when and where do you want to meet?" he asked.

"I'll message the address. Don't be late." Said the voice.

"Of course." He replied.

The line was cut. Everyone took off their headphones.

"Call traced to a PCO in an area of Panaji, Goa." Said Zain.

"So we came here for no reason?" asked Agent Akhtar.

"Let's see the message." Said Agent Khanna.

A beep came to Prakash's phone. He opened the message and showed the address written.

Plot #72, street 10, TSIIC Industrial Park, Nacharam, Hyderabad. 18th, 11:00 pm. Don't be late.

"Now it's Hyderabad." Said Zain.

"Book tickets. Now." Said Agent Rao.

He started typing. After a few minutes,

"Four hours later." He said.

While waiting for the boarding gate to open, Agent Rao got a phone call.

"Yeah, dad!" she answered.

"Updates, please." He said.

"It was a team of five. One died in an accident. They are in Hyderabad for a meeting with someone who can help them across the border. Give us two days." She said.

"All right. Remember, the priority is the LOCKER contents. Then apprehending the thieves." He said.

"Yes, sir." She said.

He cut the phone call after a slight grunt as a reply.

After reaching Hyderabad, they went in another warehouse and planned.

"All of us have to be in this. Zain, you're our eyes. The rest will be with me. I've got a few others too. We'll wait for the right minute and bust in on my order. Got it?" said Agent Rao, after they reviewed their plans.

"Yes, ma'am!" they all said.

They had scanned the area and installed cameras for Zain as well.

On that night, while everyone was getting ready,

"Ready?" asked Agent Rao after fixing a concealable microphone on Agent Kapoor.

"How the hell am I going to handle this? They knew about me, kept watch on me all this time, for the Past-I don't know." He said, sitting down with his hands on his forehead in distress.

"It's different now. We got your back. The shipment is here. Zain confirmed it. They will be here too. We'll get it all back." She said.

"Zain confirmed it, huh." He murmured.

Something's not right…

At the drop site, everyone waited.

"Agent Kapoor is approaching." Said Agent Rao through her Bluetooth.

He approached a street light that was flickering and waited for some time. It was very silent and dark with a lot of crickets chirping. Just then, he saw a flashlight flicker at a distance.

"There's someone ahead, guys." Said Agent Kapoor.

"You stay put. We need to keep our eyes on you." Said Agent Rao.

"Okay, I got it." He said.

"Zain, can you look closer ahead to where Agent Kapoor is standing?" asked Agent Rao.

"It's pretty dark but a light is visible. I can't see much." He said.

"Looks like it's useless for you, huh." Said Agent Rao.

"I'm afraid so, sorry." He said.

"It's okay, be alert." She said.

They all continued to wait patiently for their target. After a few minutes, a man appeared out of a shadowed building and walked over towards Agent Kapoor under the flickering light. He looked completely unknown.

"So! You coming here means that you are very capable of crossing the border." Said the man.

It was the same voice on the phone calls.

"You've known, huh. I thought you all forgot about me." Said Agent Kapoor.

"We never forget the best. Did you forget us?" asked the man.

"Of course not. My life is indebted to you." He said.

"Even your family?" he asked.

Prakash said nothing.

"It's okay. You deserve your freedom. If you just help us cross the border with our shipment, then we'll leave you and your family alone for good." He said.

"Really? You'll leave me alone? Just like that?" asked Agent Kapoor, getting suspicious.

"Agent Kapoor, he's the only one there. We can get him."
Said Agent Rao.

"Of course. So we can leave town now and rendezvous with the others. We'll finish the job quickly. So, what do you say?" he asked.

Shit…it's not here! The shipment's not here! We've been led into a trap! What do I do? He's not alone! Vijayanti! How can I tell you while being in front of this guy?! We're trapped!

Prakash panicked on the inside but showed a poker face of thinking to the target.

"I know something to give your decision making a push."
He said and pushed a button on a small box in his hand.

"Aah! Aah! Aah!"

Suddenly Prakash yanked out his earpiece in irritation! The earpiece suddenly gave a high screech which made him pull it out!

"I knew about the number of cops here!" said the man.

"I had no choice." He blurted out. "They found me!"

"I know your loyalty. After 2 minutes, I'll be able to get out of here. They can't hear you now so come on!" said the man. "Help me get this off!" he exclaimed while tugging the wires off himself as he rushed over to him.

"Move in now. It's clear, Agent Rao." Said Zain.

"You heard him!" said Agent Rao, relaying the instructions. Immediately the police with the LSS agents ran over to the spot! Suddenly a few were shot down! A few people from the opposing side rushed over and started shooting. Everybody took cover and shot back. One of them handed a gun to Prakash! He grabbed it and loaded it. The entire area turned into a shootout! The realization came that the bad guys were more ready for the cops!

"Let's go, Prakash!" said the man.

"Right behind you!" he said.

They took cover and ran further into the dark alley. A cop was about to shoot them when someone from their direction shot the cop right in his head. The two of them looked back to see Zain pointing the gun and holding a bag pack.

"Right on time! Let's go!" said the man to Zain.

They all got on bikes and left as one by one, cops were wounded on the ground!

"Get on!" yelled the man.

Prakash froze as he saw Agent Akhtar wounded in a corner! Suddenly Vijayanti fell to the ground! She faced his direction while holding her stomach! It was bleeding!

Vijayanti! No!

"Prakash! Get on!" shouted the man.

Suddenly, Agent Khanna rushed over to Agent Rao while clutching his arm because of a bullet and sirens were being heard from a distance!

Help's here! Vijayanti…Khanna…I'm sorry!

Prakash got on the bike behind the man quickly and rode away before anyone noticed him properly.

"No!"

Vijayanti exclaimed when she awoke seeing herself in a hospital room. She looks around and sees her phone on the table. She reaches and checks her phone to find-

3 days…I'll kill them all.

She deleted the message after seeing it.

Oh shit…

Chapter Fourteen – Still stuck?

Suddenly Vijayanti woke up from her desk. She rubbed her eyes and checked the time.

I slept for 6 hours, huh…

She started reading a file while yawning. Just then, a peon came inside.

"The Chair wants to meet you now." He said and left.

She put the file down and left while fixing her hair. She went out of the office in the LSS side building to the topmost floor of the HQ building. She went into the office after knocking the door. She enters the cabin to see the IB board member sitting. She beckoned her to sit. The LSS Director sat down in one of the chairs.

"Any updates on the case of the LSS Agents? And Prakash?" she asked.

"Umm…not much. But it seems as though a separate group of assassins must have handled it." Said Vijayanti.

"That's very possible. They are manufacturing people. Businessmen. He must have hired assassins. But how will you search for the ones?" she asked.

"I have my ways. I'll surely get it." Said Vijayanti.

"Good to know. I expect good results." Said Manisha.

"Of course, ma'am." Said the Director.

At school, a notice came on the main notice boards of the school: the hostel ground floor and the school main building.

NOTICE - December

Final semester Examinations for all classes will be held from February 20th onwards. By 10th February, all projects, notes, etc., must be submitted to respective subject teachers. The Principal will give final checking to them.

1. *Class 10 and 12 will be given an orientation about their board examination centres.*

2. *Strict action will be taken against those who disrupt the study hours of others in the school, hostels or the canteen.*

3. *Sankranti holidays are from 11th to 16th January.*

4. *Nobody is to disturb the army. Threats are coming along the border so they are here for our safety.*

That is all.

Everybody saw the notice, staff and students, and the talk of the few days was the notice.

Meanwhile, Simran was in her room with Radhika. More than a couple of weeks had passed and the cell phone was almost hacked completely. They kept looking anxiously at the loading bar. 90%....95%...99%...

"Finally! Yes!" exclaimed Radhika.

"Oh thank goodness. So much time!" said Simran in exhaustion.

Simran pulled her chair near the desk and typed some more and pressed enter. The phone was unlocked. It asked for the passkey. In a few seconds of loading, a 6-digit number appeared on the laptop screen. Radhika typed it in and it was accepted! She searched inside.

"Anything?" asked Simran.

"No! It's empty!" said Radhika.

"Check properly!" said Simran.

She continued opening various applications to find them empty. Finally, she opened the message inbox and found it to be empty. She went to the trash folder to find one message deleted. She opened it.

"Oh yes!! I knew it!" said Radhika, happily.

"What does it say?" asked Simran.

"See!" she said, showing the phone to her.

Verification Address: #23, Patan Durbar Square, Kathmandu.

Simran immediately searched the address. She also searched images of the place and showed.

"There is a five floor building. It's a depot for trucks. So many trucks go out of there every day!" said Simran.

"Oh great! That's just great! Another dead end! It's impossible for anyone to look there! We don't know where all those shipments went!" said Radhika, angrily.

"I don't know what to do now…" said Simran.

"I need a break from this stuff! I'm going and writing my chemistry record!" said Radhika.

"Go ahead. I'm going to think." Said Simran.

"Simran, let it go for now. We don't have access everywhere-" Started Radhika.

"I'm not leaving this!" said Simran, getting annoyed.

Radhika was taken aback.

"I'm not giving up." Said Simran and resumed typing.

Radhika left in frustration. Simran continued thinking, searching the internet and checking. She was going to miss duty but she had to go because Arjun was still in his hostel room taking it easy and recovering. She still took her laptop there and was thinking and typing.

She returned to the hostels after duty and dinner and saw a lot of noise on the ground floor! She went ahead in the common ground floor corridor to find a TV on in a room with many people inside occupying the sofas, bed and chairs. They were watching cricket and many others were drinking and eating snacks. They were consisting of classes 9 to 12 students mostly. Simran peered inside and saw Shreya and Neerav eating and watching the match. Nikhil and Natasha were drinking with others. The room reeked with Alcohol, cheese from pizza and a slight amount of smoke from a cigarette or two somewhere. A couple of teachers were there too with a few staff members.

The nurse passed by the room, showed a disturbed and annoyed look, greeted Simran and left. Simran saw the match playing on the TV.

At one time,

"Dad! Stop!" said Simran.

She looked 8 to 9 years old then.

"What's the problem?" he asked.

"Ugh, whose side are you on?" said one boy, annoyingly on the sofa.

He was at least 17 to 18 years old.

"Hey, I'm with India!" said her dad.

"Oh yeah? Then what's the idea of yelling 'Out' at our wicket going?" said a lady coming out of the kitchen with a bowl of popcorn.

"Come on! Paying extra for this HD channel, we deserve an interesting match!" said her father.

"I just want to win." Murmured the boy.

"Yeah, me too!" said Simran.

"You'll get an interesting one." Said her dad.

"Mom, look!" said the boy.

"We'll win, *beta*! You, mister, stop that!" said the lady.

Simran shook her head pushing away the memory. She rubbed her eyes and left upstairs to her room and sat down at her desk. Indira then came to her door.

"Simran, your turn to watch the LOCKER is coming after a while. Who do you want to be with?" she asked.

"I'm not in the mood for anyone! You're always putting me with Raghav or Nikhil. I'd rather be alone!" said Simran, annoyed.

"Sure? That night? Alone?" asked Indira.

"Uh…yeah…why?" asked Simran.

"The final match is then. We all are going to watch! And I guess, you and Arjun are only there for extra duty tomorrow. But Arjun is still under bedrest." Said Indira.

"Radhika?" asked Simran.

"Uh…"

"On second thought, it's okay! Just don't tell anything to Arjun. I'll do it." Said Simran, still annoyed.

"Okay, bye!" she said and left.

Simran continued typing and searching.

No need to get Radhika. She wanted to hang around with Gaurav. Whatever, I can handle a night alone.

The match continued till 12:30 till everything ended. Everyone left to their rooms and went to sleep. Simran was awake till then still thinking.

A while later, Shreya entered the room. She closed the door and saw Simran still awake with her hand massaging her forehead in irritation. Her laptop was off. A folder with a few pictures was on the table.

"What happened?" asked Shreya.

"It's not fair! I'm not getting any leads! Whatever I think of, it's useless! It's always a dead end!" said Simran, getting fed up.

She put her head down on the table in frustration.

"Come on, you'll always get something. I can't help you because I don't want to be involved in anything." Said Shreya.

"Nobody can help me." Said Simran.

Suddenly, something caught Shreya's eyes! She opened her eyes wider at the desk. She scrambled and pulled out the picture under Simran's arm and held it closer. She observed it even more closely. Simran got up and noticed her expression with curiosity.

"You know this guy?" asked Simran.

She didn't reply.

"Who all did you show this to?" asked Shreya.

"Everyone here. Why?" asked Simran.

"What did Neerav say about this?" asked Shreya.

"He said that he doesn't know this guy." Said Simran.

She nodded. She went and closed the curtains and bolted the door.

"Who is this guy?" asked Simran.

"Search for Rohit." She said.

"Assassin Rohit? Your ex Rohit?" asked Simran.

"Try for a match." She said, giving the photo and sitting down on the bed close to her.

After some typing and pressing enter loading the photographs together.

"It's a 100% match." Said Simran.

"Oh god. I knew it!" she said, covering her mouth.

"Well, something now! He was seen nearby here with the robber." Said Simran.

"Oh my god. We're screwed!" she said.

"Why?" she asked.

"You don't understand. He's an excellent tracker! If he finds me…oh god. I should, I should go home or-" She said, in fear.

"Hey, hey, hey! He was in town! His job might have been over when the LOCKER was robbed! It's okay!" said Simran, reassuring her.

"I don't know! But what lead does this give you now?" asked Shreya.

Simran thought for a moment and smacked her forehead.

"That's right! Still nothing! God damn it!" said Simran.

"It's okay, you've gotten further, at least!" said Shreya. "Good night."

"Good night." Said Simran.

Shreya went to bed and slept turning off her lamp. Simran thought for some more time and then turned off her light too.

What do I do now?

The next few days, Simran spend the day in her room still thinking about the investigation. Radhika stayed in her room completing her notes with Gaurav. Everybody else were downstairs building up their cricket fever.

In the afternoon, Simran went to the boys' side of the hostel and climbed the stairs till the top floor with a file in her hand. She went to the last room and knocked on the door.

"Who is it?" came Arjun's voice from inside.

"It's me! Simran." She said.

"Oh, you! Come in and close the door after you." He said.

She came in and closed the door after her. She turned around to see him in his bed sitting upright with a pillow behind him.

"You never visit; Miss know it all! Feeling lonely at duty?" he asked, while rubbing his eyes and fixing his hair.

"As if!" – he gave a look – "Okay, fine." she said, still standing.

"Well, since we're both bored, sit down." He said, giving a yawn.

She took a chair and put it near where Arjun was sitting and sat down.

"So…what's up with you?" he asked.

"I, uh…I haven't been sleeping for a couple of days. And… I'm reaching dead ends in the case." She said.

"Huh…That's rare." He said.

"I can't find anything. Prakash and his team have disappeared. And he was working with this guy." Said Simran, showing a picture of Rohit.

"Hey…he once bought bombs from me. Only grenades." Said Arjun, while covering the mouth and forehead of the picture.

"Really?" she said.

"Yeah…" he said.

"How long ago did you finish this business of yours?" she asked.

"Long time…um…three or four years." He said.

I'm not telling you!

"Anyway, this guy was seen with the thief. And get this: he's Shreya's ex." She said.

"What?! Are you serious?" he asked.

"Yeah…still no use. He's as much of a ghost as they are." She said.

"You know, you forgot to read the Chennai report. Do you know what it said?" he asked.

"What? You had it all this time?" she asked.

"Yeah…nobody knows I did." He said, while pointing to his desk drawer.

She immediately opened it and took it out while closing the drawer and started looking through it.

"I thought we were going to share everything with each other, asshole! My god!" she said, while flipping pages.

"We just agreed to that a week ago. I forgot." He said.

"I'm resisting to punch you." She said.

He chuckled.

"The package was coming in three boxes but it was separately sent from different places. This was the one from Chennai. The contents were bombs with some chemical in them. Some chemical with Sulphur and Chlorine. They looked European. They were very old." He said.

"Hmm…but we heard that it had guns and what-not." she said.

"Well, it wasn't. So?" he asked.

"I'm still not going to be able to find any clue with this." Said Simran.

"Nothing on the internet, huh." He said.

"Yeah…I don't know where else to look." She said.

"You know, it's irrelevant but the most hidden away information is in the LOCKERs. Too bad, we can't find anything in them." He said.

"Yeah…" – the bell rang – "Oh well, I'll go for duty. Thanks." She said.

"For what?" he asked.

"For talking to me. See you." She said and left his room.

She came to see me for help…indirectly.

Simran continued walking in the corridor. She went to her room and searched the CBI Chennai database of analyses. She found the package they had recovered. She hacked into the complete details.

Let's see…the chemical…huh? Sulphur mustard?

She searched the name and found details.

Hmm…European history…hmm…North Sea?

She then paused and searched in the news.

Over 200 vintage WWI chemical bombs found in 2014 are reported to be missing from the past three months?! That should be it!

Just then, the bell rang. Simran left for duty.

Chapter Fifteen – Inside the LOCKER!

After dinner, Simran went to the LOCKER while everybody was in the TV room watching the match. She stayed there with her laptop and worked while the basement doors shut for the night with the defence personnel leaving. After a while of still thinking and searching, she fell asleep.

The next morning, Simran woke up abruptly and looked around. It was still early and the sun did not rise yet. She was still in the LOCKER corridor in the basement. She gets up and stretches. Then she walks over to the open door of the LOCKER with the red laser beams and stands in front of it thinking about the case still. She then sighs, goes back and opens her laptop again to search for something which popped into her mind. She typed and pressed enter to find details of the LOCKERs.

So every LOCKER has files of different categories. So LOCKER 02 is…okay…building plans…then LOCKER 17… homicides…LOCKER 01…Historic-Hmmm…No! Don't get so into this! There is no way that I am going to go inside there and see…but, Radhika set the lasers. The door is still there… No! Simran, control yourself! Arh! This is so infuriating!

She continued debating for a while.

I know that the Supreme Court confiscated our reserve of Sulphur mustard in 2008 or 2009. It was supposed to be destroyed but we still kept it. Maybe they kept it somewhere in the country. But that would be risky and Prakash is collecting it. If it was somewhere in the country, the information would be in LOCKER 01. Historic confiscations. That's what it says.

She put her hands on her forehead in frustration.

Okay, that's it!

She shuts her laptop, gets up while taking it and goes to the meeting room. She opens a few drawers and finds a couple of cables. She then goes out and pulls out the electricity board at the LOCKER entrance and connects her cables in. She then connects the cables to the laptop and starts typing various codes.

Oh, Radhika…if only you could make this more secure…

She finished and the lasers immediately vanished. It was done. She placed her laptop down and took a step inside. She grabbed the knob of the inner door.

Okay, just look for that one thing then get out of there and put the lasers back on before anyone notices. Okay…

She took a deep breath, turned the knob of the door and pulled. It slowly opened with a creak that echoed the corridor.

Shit!

She went back out to look around. The main basement door was still locked. She sighed with relief and went back inside. She pulled the door a little more. It was a very old door so it got slightly jammed. She went inside the room and froze. She gaped at the size of the room.

How big is this LOCKER?! Is every LOCKER this big?! Wow… this looks so much bigger than the library…amazing!

She walked around, while covering her nose to avoid the dust, gaping around at each shelf being huge. The shelves were a little taller than her and a foot and a half wide. Each of the were divided into five rows and columns. In the squares made by the shelves, there were many files stacked on each other and were adjusted tightly in each square making them very difficult to pull out.

How will I find-

A fallen shelf at the corner of the room caught Simran's eye. She went and checked which shelf was slightly empty.

These files didn't fall even when the shelf fell so hard. This must be the one which had the missing folder.

She bent and pulled out all the folders displaced from that square and blew on them to get most of the dust off. She then started looking inside each of them.

So one of the places is at the border in West Bengal. Hmm…

After a few minutes, she kept the files and started walking back to the entrance. While walking,

The country surely seals a lot of stuff...I should go...enough looking around.

She was just about to step outside when she saw a box in the corner. It was strange because that was the only box that was in this LOCKER. It was written roughly with a CD marker 'LSS 1027'. She looks inside and finds a few papers and a file. She sees them and looks into the file.

Hey...a list of Prakash's family...hmm...let's see...deceased,

She turned a page.

Deceased.

She turned a page.

Missing…oh so old…definitely deceased.

She read through further till she reached a certain family member which made her drop the file in shock.

Oh shit…

She immediately put back the papers and the file in the box, closed it and shoved it to a corner. She got up and left outside, grabbed her laptop and set the lasers again looking the same as before. She unplugged the cables, put the board back on and hit it to fix it firmly on the wall. She then went to the meeting room and kept back those cables in the drawer. She went outside and sat in a corner with her laptop waiting for the main basement door to unlock.

During break, Simran was only glued to her laptop. Radhika was reading a textbook next to her but constantly drooping down. She was sleepy.

"Were you watching the entire match last night?" asked Simran.

"Oh, yeah. Gaurav and I went." She said.

"Interesting…" said Simran.

A pause followed.

"You used to like cricket, Simran. It's no harm in watching a match." Said Radhika.

"I was focused on the case anyway. Watching a match would divert my attention." Simran replied.

Radhika closed her textbook and pushed it to a side.

"You sound like you've progressed." She said, folding her arms.

"Oh hell yeah, I did." Said Simran, with a smirk on her face, a smirk almost as large as a smile.

Radhika noticed and realized that Simran was…happy.

"Stop staring if you want to know what I've found out." Said Simran.

The smirk wiped off her face. Radhika put her textbook in her bag and scooted her chair closer to Simran. Simran did not tell her anything about her trip to the LOCKER, let alone mention the box with Prakash's details in it. Radhika's face turned from poker to shocked in an instant when she heard about the connection of Prakash to chemical bombing. Upon realizing, Radhika immediately looked in another direction to contain her emotions! Simran concluded and showed her the laptop.

"We have to go check this place out. We can get some lead there." Said Simran.

Radhika said nothing and kept looking at the place.

"So when shall we go?" asked Simran.

Radhika sighed.

"Come on, this is big!" started Simran.

"Yes, it's atrocious. Just tell the Director about it. We shouldn't go or else we might get caught up in something dangerous." said Radhika.

"Come on! We are already in a dangerous situation! The Director said that we should investigate ourselves a bit and-"Simran started.

"Simran, just see the gravity of the situation! This is about Prakash planning something with his terrorist organisation and collecting the most dangerous banned chemical weaponry! What is there not to tell ma'am?! I can't go with you to find something that bad!" she said, angrily.

Simran silently listened.

"I'm sorry, but it might be dangerous." She said.

There was a pause.

"On the contrary, it might even be a hunch. We should still go. We'd need some proof to show ma'am, right?" said Simran.

"But the LOCKER is still open. The sealing guy did not come yet. What if he comes while we are gone?" she asked.

"We will go early in the morning and be back in the afternoon or evening. He will still be there." She said.

"Fine...but don't you start involving Arjun." She said.

"Promise."

"Okay, for now. No Gaurav either." Said Simran.

"Okay. We'll go after exams. They'll start next week. We'll then have a lot of time off till April. Let's see what we find." Said Radhika.

"Got it." Said Simran.

"No telling Arjun. I'm warning you." Said Radhika.

"It's okay, I won't. He'll never find out anyway since he's still recovering." Said Simran and left.

A couple of days later, while walking back to the hostels,

Should I go see him? No, I'll keep my distance. Things have gotten complicated and I have to solve this or else I won't be able to sleep…

"Simran!" called out someone from behind.

She suddenly startled out of her thoughts and turned around to see Gaurav. He rushed over, grabbed her arm and pulled her to a corner of the main school building.

"What happened?" she asked.

"You tell me." – shoving a crumpled piece of paper in her hand – "You know where I found it." He said.

She held the paper but didn't dare unfold it.

"See what it is, Simran." He said, sternly.

She slowly opened the crumpled piece of paper and immediately crushed it back into a crumpled ball again.

"What all did Radhika tell you?" she asked.

"She just told me that the guy who put this missing poster of you wants your head. Possibly hers." He said.

She slightly nodded after peeking around to check if nobody was there.

"Should I be worried about this? Or should I be pissed off about you two going somewhere without me?" he asked, folding his arms.

"Seriously now, I can't even trust my best friend! How much does she like you?" said Simran, annoyed.

"Like me? No, don't change the subject here. You got some valuable and dangerous information and we can visit the place- "he started.

"Oh come on! She told you this?! Who else is going to find out now?!" she said, infuriated.

"Hey, I'm not going to tell anyone here! We three are together in this!" – staring at her and putting a hand on her shoulder – "Please stop pushing me out. I promise I won't get hurt!" he said.

She gave one long look at him then sighed and looked down. Suddenly, she put one arm around his neck and pulled him into a quick hug.

"I'm just worried about you. Radhika is caring for someone other than me and herself. I'm still trying to get used to it." She said.

He didn't say anything.

"You've got her back, right?" she asked.

"Always." He said.

"AHEM!"

Suddenly they pulled away and turned around to see Radhika standing there tapping her foot.

"Sorry!" – taking a step back – "All yours! We'll leave next week after the last exam. I'll give details later." Said Simran and immediately left.

Chapter Sixteen – Not abandoned!

Their last exam finished and the three top 50 agents finalised the next investigative place. Early in the morning, on one cloudy day in the ending of March, Simran got up and took her bag pack already stuffed with her laptop, tablet, a gun with ammo and another pair of clothes, sneaked out of her room and left downstairs from the hostels. She was supposed to meet Gaurav and Radhika at the West gate in another ten minutes as she checked her watch. It was 6:15am.

As she went towards the back gate of the hostels, she saw the surveillance room unlocked.

What the-I locked it yesterday!

She slowly went towards the door and peeked inside. She couldn't get a good look and she went inside and quickly closed the door without a sound.

"What are you doing up so early?"

It was Arjun. He was sitting on a chair. He got up and leaned on the table with his arms folded.

"What are you doing here?" she asked.

"I'm allowed to roam around now." He said.

"I know but what are you doing so early in here?" she asked.

"Last night you said that they finally replaced the door so I came to see. Now back to you: Where are you going?" he asked.

"I got a lead nearby in a village of West Bengal. At the border." She said.

"Congrats, you got something." He said.

There was a pause.

"How did you get it?" he asked.

What should I say now? Um…

"I don't know; it suddenly came to me." She said.

"Ah, good for you." He said.

"Thanks. Well, I'd better go now. Radhika and Gaurav are waiting for me. We'll be back before duty." She said and turned around.

"Simran!" – she turned back around – "I hope you know what you're doing." He said.

"I got this, Arjun. You just focus on duty and recovering. Bye." She said, turned around and left the surveillance room. She went to the West gate to find Radhika and Gaurav on two bikes waiting. Simran got on the bike behind Radhika and they left the campus. They reached the main highway and drove for a while. After an hour, they stopped at a roadside tea stall and rested themselves.

"How much further?" asked Radhika.

"Quite a lot. If we want to be back before Princi gets back, then we have to be quick about it. She will drive into the campus tomorrow at 11:25am sharp. If we are late then the others might tell off on us. Like Nikhil." Said Gaurav.

"Look, we know the way, we will get there, check the place for anything then leave. It won't take much time." Said Simran.

They finished their light breakfast and started driving on the highway. Simran drove with Radhika sitting behind her. Gaurav drove alone on another bike. A couple of hours later, they stopped to stretch their legs. This time, Gaurav got tired and sat behind Radhika while Simran drove his bike. The backdrop of the highways was all normal. Just a few agricultural fields, tiny towns, many hills with still a cloudy atmosphere. They reached the border of Assam and West Bengal and crossed it in a few hours.

Finally, at 2:50pm after their last pit stop, they reached a small village and passed through it. The villagers looked at them once then returned to their daily chores. In the farther distance was a small hill. While going closer, the trio could spot a small, concrete-like hut at the base. It looked old and abandoned. The hut was just in concrete colour without any paint. They parked their bikes right in front and went towards it. there was only one door and one window in the front face. The rest of the walls were closed. It definitely seemed like a place to store chemicals.

As they edged closer, they noticed the door slightly open. Simran raised her hand slightly to halt. She examined the door carefully and noticed it being wooden and frail. There was only a huge chunk of door missing…one that had the bolt and handle.

"How in the hell can a door to a sealed stored chemical be broken so easily?" wondered Radhika.

"I thought it would have a code or something." Said Gaurav.

"Yeah, I thought we need to hack it in or something. This is just plain stupid." Said Simran, stepping back from the broken-down door.

"This just means one thing." Said Radhika, shoving past them and going towards the door.

She stopped a metre away in front and rotated her foot. Then she changed and rotated her other foot.

"What are you about to do?" asked Gaurav, confused.

"Just get back." She said, without giving a look.

Simran pulled him back a couple of feet. Radhika hopped a little in one place warming up then stopped. Suddenly she leaped and gave one hard right kick and broke down the rest of the door into three to four pieces! They fell with a thud inside on the hard, dusty floor. They stepped inside to see the room completely empty. Not a trace of…anything was seen.

"This place was a rendezvous point for the package." Said Radhika.

"But this place was a store house for the chemicals! I searched a trustable information centre." asked Simran.

"Maybe it's somewhere nearby?" suggested Gaurav.

"Okay. Then let's scour the area." Said Simran.

They left the hut and trekked up the hill behind it. After a while, they reached the top and stood on a huge rock. Cool wind blew at their faces. The whole village could be seen from that peak.

"I found something!" exclaimed Radhika.

She looked in the southern direction with respect to the small concrete hut. Simran and Gaurav turned around and looked in the direction down where Radhika pointed. Down below the hill had an abandoned looking factory. It was quite large and surprisingly, covered in total black as the trio noticed upon reaching it. They casually hiked all the way. As they walked towards the entrance, Simran quickly pulled them behind the wall.

"The factory has people inside. But not the workers." She said.

"Should we split up?" asked Radhika.

Gaurav peeked in from their side of the wall to see two well-built men talking to each other with guns in their pockets. He peeked in more to find a few more well-built guyseverywhere. One the balconies, ground, roof, etc. they looked very dangerous.

"It's too risky!" whispered Gaurav.

"Then should we come back later?" asked Radhika.

"No, we don't have much time. We'll have to sneak in." said Simran.

"Are you crazy?! Look at them!" whispered Gaurav.

"All right, let's go back to the hut. I left my bag there." Said Simran.

They sneak away and go back around the hill to the hut. Gaurav and Radhika sat down bored on the dirt road while Simran kept rummaging through her bag pack trying to search for something.

Come on! Where is it?!

She kept searching.

Yes! I knew I brought it!

She took out two small cameras of hers, the same ones that were utilised in Chennai, and handed one to Radhika.

Then she handed over her laptop to Gaurav after she typed something.

"Radhika and I will sneak in together. It won't take long for her to get some pictures and me to plant this bug on one camera. Gaurav, you just press install when it comes. Automatically, it will create an entrance for me. I will come back and hack it. Okay?" Simran explained.

"Fine. But don't take too long." said Gaurav.

They left the hut while Gaurav stayed with the open laptop. The two of them went around the hill and sneaked up to the entrance again. They hid behind a wall and Simran slowly peeked inside while Radhika inspected the condition of her camera. Simran spotted a few men roaming around casually in the open ground. She pulled back and pointed to go right along the wall to the back. Radhika understood and followed her. They walked slowly with their backs touching the wall and turned right. They reached the back entrance and Simran peered inside. She couldn't see anybody nearby. They went inside the back entrance and were inside the premises. They went left into an old door inside the factory.

It was dark inside but they had entered a huge hall where numerous looming machines were there. The machines looked old and dusty.

"How long ago was this abandoned?" wondered Radhika.

"We can't stick around to find out. Come on." Said Simran. They went across the room carefully without making a sound. Simran slightly opened the door and peeked inside to see a small room with a table and a couple of chairs. A cheap tube light was on and at least ten people were inside discussing something. Simran placed the bug on the door and backed away. She turned to Radhika, put a finger on her lips and motioned her to follow Simran. She nodded and they left quickly. They walked out the hall and onto the ground.

"There were ten people in there, I don't recognise anyone. I put the bug on the door so let's just go quickly!" said Simran. They went out the back entrance from where they entered from and after some distance they ran as fast as they could away from the place. They went around the hill and to the old hut. Gaurav was sitting inside and the laptop was still on.

"Did you do it?" asked Radhika.

"Why are you back? I didn't get any signal from that bug!" said Gaurav.

"What do you mean? I put it very carefully!" said Simran.

She goes to the laptop and searches for signals. Again she tries typing a few codes but it was of no use. Something was wrong. After trying for some more time, she stopped at realising. Gaurav and Radhika were still puzzled.

"We have to leave. We've been caught." Said Simran, frantically slamming down the laptop and stuffing it in her bag pack.

Gaurav grabbed the keys to the bikes and tossed one of them to Radhika. She caught it immediately and they went through the broken doorway outside. They quickly ran over to their bikes but suddenly heard gun shots from a distance! They turned around while taking cover and saw at least five to six people coming running down the hills with guns! The trio were trapped! Immediately, Simran took out her gun and retaliated with a few shots while Gaurav and Radhika went and started the bikes!

"AAHH!!!!"

Simran caught a bullet on her leg! She collapsed but was still shooting!

"Go!" yelled out Simran.

Gaurav and Radhika got down and pulled her up. Gaurav put Simran's arm around his shoulder and quickly helped her limp away towards the bikes but the people already reached and surrounded them! Guns pointed at them from all directions!

"Hands up!" said one well-built man in the front, aiming with his AK 47.

Radhika's hands were up. Gaurav and Simran did the same but Simran still felt pain. After trying to balance herself, she fell hard to the ground holding her leg in pain! A few guys pointed their guns down at her!

"Well, if it isn't you two!"

The leader came forward after saying that.

"You! Uh…um…" Radhika exclaimed but forgot his name.

"Aroop…" Simran said, in pain.

"Guns down, they're friends. Help her. Come on, guys! Let's go back to the factory." He said and went.

Immediately, two of the men put their guns back on their shoulders and picked up Simran. She was supported by putting her arms around their shoulders. Two more guys took the bikes and rode them towards the factory. After they all reached, Simran was immediately put on the table in the room. Aroop turned on a torch and showed it on the wound.

"It's okay. The bullet's not there. Put a bandage on her, one of you." Said Aroop and left the room.

Radhika and Gaurav watched while Simran was getting the bandage tied. After it was done, Simran thanked him and he nodded his head and left the room. The three of them were alone.

"So you know the guy?" asked Gaurav.

"Yeah, we do. But what is he involved in now?" wondered Radhika.

"Well, one thing is for certain." Said Simran.

"What?" they asked in unison.

"We'll be away from school for a while." she said.

Chapter Seventeen – Nepal?!

After an hour or so, a man came and called them out. Radhika helped Simran up and they went out into the hall with abandoned looms. The others were present as well.

"So, were you supposed to find us or you just happened to stumble upon this place?" asked Aroop.

"We came to look for something else." Said Simran.

"And you thought we might know something so you put a bug. Where did a top 50 kid like you even get it?" asked one guy.

"I made it." said Radhika.

He spoke no more.

"Well, you have come at the right time, you know?" said Aroop.

The trio were puzzled.

"You came to look for the packages stolen from evidences which your team recovered in Chennai, right? Since they are rightfully yours to see." asked Aroop.

It was stolen?! Prakash got that too!

"Seeing your reaction tells us that you did not know. Anyway, the LSS Director contacted me and my team about it. The case is under our jurisdiction now." He said.

"Oh…" said Radhika.

"But, we definitely need all the help we could get. So you are in, right?" said Aroop.

They looked to each other. Gaurav and Radhika looked at Simran.

"We don't have a choice, do we?" said Radhika, uneasy.

"Agent Simran Khanna, you do owe me a favour for not killing you. I was promoted recently too." Said Aroop.

Simran didn't reply.

"Come on, kid! You'll get a lot of closure on this case, on me and...the one looking for you...maybe..." he said, tempting her.

She looked up at that.

"Yeah, we're in." she said.

"Great! Well, let's get down to business. Let's see what you know first." Said Aroop.

Back at school, Arjun was at the surveillance room. He didn't leave there. He just sat there and brooded.

I wish I could've gone with her. But she should be back by now. But if she's back now, then she found no lead. If she isn't back, then either she's in trouble or she found something. Hope that know-it-all is okay. And Gaurav and Radhika. It's getting more dangerous. That LOCKER isn't closed yet too.

"Hey, what are you doing here?" asked Nikhil, coming inside.

Not him again…

"Nothing. What's up?" asked Arjun.

"Simran, Radhika and Gaurav are missing at duty. Where did they go?" asked Nikhil.

"I don't know; I didn't see them since morning." Said Arjun.

"You should be in bed, you know." He said.

"I've been in bed for a month." He said.

"Anything you know on Prakash?" he asked.

Always meddling in only these things…he doesn't talk about anything else.

"Nope." He replied.

"Okay…" he said and left.

I feel so weak…

"*Simran!*" – *she turned back around* – "*I hope you know what you're doing.*" *He had said.*

"*I got this, Arjun. You just focus on duty and recovering. Bye.*" *She had said, turned around and left the surveillance room.*

He remembered further.

Before leaving for Chennai, in the meeting room,

"*So, in a way, me not keeping an eye on you will jeopardize the mission? Come on! Don't act so weak!*" *Simran had said.*

"*I'm not weak! This rarely happens and I'm really having a problem-* "*he started.*

"*You can't be serious. All of a sudden, have you stopped believing yourself or something?*" *Simran had asked.*

He further remembered again.

"*Sorry that we couldn't get her.*" *He had said, in the warehouse in Chennai.*

"*It's my fault. I didn't expect her to be this good.*" *She had said.*

"No, I screwed up again. I let her get away. Then she set the entire dockyard on fire!" he had said.

"It's okay…" she had said, feeling his forehead to check for a fever.

He came back to the present.

I can't sit around and do nothing. I must fix myself.

Indira was at the east gate of the school with Neerav and suddenly her phone rang. She picked up and looked.

This guy? Ugh, what does he want?

"Hello?" answered Indira.

"I need a favour, Indu." Said Arjun from the surveillance room.

"I don't do favours for assholes like you." She said.

"I'm serious. I need to get better." He said.

"Why? You have others to depend on." She said.

"Look, Simran might not be back for a while, okay? And I need to get better before she gets back." He said.

"Huh, where did she go?" she asked.

"I don't know, okay? Just please help me out here." He said.

"What do you want?" she asked.

"Put someone in the surveillance for the next couple of weeks. Please." He said.

"Woah…you just said please. Wow, you're serious about her, huh." She said.

"Think what you want. Are you doing it or not?" he asked.

"Yeah, sure. I'll get it covered." She said.

"Thanks. And please don't mention this to Nikhil." He said.

"Sure…get better." She said and cut the call.

This guy…but where did they go?!

At the factory, the trio finished giving their investigative report. All of them were shocked. Aroop the most.

"So all that…you were able to deduce with a computer?" asked one guy.

"Yeah." Said Radhika.

"So our common problem is where to find his hideout. The place where all the shipments went to is still mysterious." Said Aroop.

"There was only one thing that three packages intercepted at the truck depot in Kathmandu. Still, hundreds of trucks go out and come in every day." Said Gaurav.

"Okay, we'll stop here. I'll make some calls and see what I can get. You all can go eat something and get some rest." Said Aroop. "Disperse!"

Everybody left outside to the ground and saw others bringing take-out food from the nearby village. Within a few minutes, everybody quickly ate their shares and went to bed. One man escorted the top 50 trio upstairs to three empty beds in a room. He left them alone.

"What a day…" said Simran, sitting on a bed.

"You can say that again." Said Radhika, sitting down on a bed.

"Well, I'll keep watch. You get some rest." Said Gaurav.

"There's no need. They could've killed us as soon as they saw us. Chill out, Gaurav." Said Radhika.

"No, he's right. Gaurav, take first watch. I'll go next." Said Simran.

"No, you rest. I and Gaurav will take turns. That leg of yours has to get better." Said Radhika.

"Okay, thanks." Said Simran.

"Good night." Said Gaurav and went outside.

The rest of the night went on. Simran slept soundly while Radhika and Gaurav took turns in keeping watch.

The next morning, everyone met after breakfast in the hall with the abandoned looms.

"We all have to leave for Nepal tomorrow. Another back up team sent from HQ will meet us at the border. So pack up everything." Announced Aroop.

WHAT?! NEPAL?!

"You three, come with me. We'll go buy some clothes for you guys. Now." Said Aroop.

"Woah!! Wait a second!" exclaimed Radhika.

They all stopped to see the shocked faces of the three of them.

"We never left the country! We can't go just like that!" she said.

"And why can't you?!" asked one guy.

They didn't say anything.

"Oh…I get it. Your in-charge doesn't know you're here. So what? You owe me a favour. You promised to help. And in turn, I give you closure." Said Aroop.

"Yes, we did…but…" said Gaurav, hesitant.

"Look, please let us go back to our school. We have to go back." Said Radhika, requesting.

"Khanna…you won't receive an opportunity like this again. We could hit the jackpot with our team up. Don't you want that?" he asked, tempting them.

"Simran, we have to leave- "started Radhika.

"No, Radhika, this is more important. It's okay, Aroop. We're in all the way." She said.

"Great. Now let's go." He said.

They left with Aroop and two other guys.

Meanwhile, at the school, Indira and Nikhil were reported to the Principal's cabin together. They were made to wait outside for a while.

Simran…it's been a day. Where the hell did you go? The school is in a vulnerable state, how could you suddenly make a trip like that without telling me?

Indira thought deeply.

"I told you before." Said Nikhil, suddenly.

"What?" she asked.

"Princi must have found out about them missing from duty. Even when I didn't tell her." He said, chuckling.

"Oh, why the sudden helpfulness?" she asked, with a hint of sarcasm.

"As much as I hate them, I know why they left." He said.

"Tell me then, let's see if you are right." She said.

"They went for investigations of Kapoor enterprise." – seeing her widened eyes – "I won't rat them out. But I want to know what they've found or else I will tell Princi." He said.

She sighed and frowned in disappointment.

"What?" he asked.

"There is always a catch with you. You never do anything good for free, huh?" she said.

"When it comes to them, that's how I'll be." He said.

"Why do you hate her so much? Is it because she's close to Arjun?" asked Indira.

He looked away.

"Why should that even matter to you? Are you jealous of that too?" she asked.

"I'm not jealous of her- "he started.

"Oh please! I'm not a fool. Just because we were never friends doesn't mean I don't know you well." she said.

"Look, she is a bad influence on him. She uses him. I want her away from him. He can't do what he wants when she's around- "he started.

"You mean he can't do what you want. And his side deals?" She said.

He was wide-eyed at that.

"I'm not dumb. I know why he sneaks out all the time. When will that end? Will it?" she asked.

"You won't understand. He's drifting away from me to her. He's my best friend. And she's keeping him away from us." He said.

"She does no such thing!" she said, angrily.

Just then, the peon called them inside and they went in. they stood in front of her while she was signing a couple of files.

"Agent Jaiswal and Agent Patel. I called you here because I finally received word from HQ that a couple of agents will come to seal the LOCKER. They arrive in a couple of hours directly here. Before duty, make sure to disable the current security of Agent Chopra so that they can seal it. Understood?" instructed Agent Rao.

"Oh, for that. Yes, ma'am!" said Nikhil.

"Were you expecting something else?" asked the Principal, suspiciously.

"No, ma'am. It's just that we almost forgot about them. Thank you for informing. We will complete this task." Said Indira, covering him.

"Good, you can leave now." She said.

They left the cabin and were in the corridor walking.

"So, since we probably still won't tell her, what do you suppose we do now?" asked Nikhil.

She was silently thinking.

"Well, if you got no ideas then I can go back and tell Princi-"he said.

"Shut up about this! I know what to do!" she said.

"Oh really? What are you going to do?" he asked.

"I'll see you later." She said and left to the hostels running.

She ran all the way and went to the boys' side of the hostels. She quickly climbed the stairs to the topmost floor and went to see a room locked.

Oh come on! Where can you possibly be now?! Wait...ahaa!

She went back downstairs and walked straight to the hostel gym to see Arjun running on a treadmill alone. She goes inside and presses a button which slowed and finally stopped the treadmill.

"Hey! I'm kind of busy here! -"he started.

"Oh, you'd wish!" she replied, stingily.

"All right!" – getting down and sitting on a bench while grabbing his bottle – "What's wrong?" he asked, taking a gulp of water.

"Agents are coming to seal the LOCKER in less than three hours! How can I disable Radhika's security without her?!" said Indira.

"Shit!" he said.

"We are lucky that Princi doesn't know yet! Do something! Did Simran really not tell you when she was coming back?!" said Indira, frantically.

"I don't know what happened to her. She was supposed to come back on the very same day!" he said.

"Don't you call her? Talk to her?!" she asked.

"She doesn't pick up. So does Radhika!" he said.

"This is on you! You better do something! Keep trying them! Call Gaurav! Call them! You got two and a half hours!" she said.

"How dare you put this on me?!" he said.

"You could have stopped them! You were up that early! Deal with this! That security has to be disabled before they get here!" she said and stormed out.

"But Indu!" he called out but she was long gone.

Dammit, Simran!

Arjun went to his room immediately and started calling Simran. She didn't pick up. He called Radhika and Gaurav next but they also did not pick up.

Oh, come on! Please please please! Anybody pick up!

He continued calling for hours till he frustratingly flopped down on his bed and put his face in his pillow while yelling in it. Just then, his phone started ringing. He picked up.

"Hello?" asked a voice.

"It's me, Arjun! My sim card broke." He said.

"Arjun?!" asked Simran on the other line.

"Oh, thank goodness, Miss know-it-all! - "he replied.

"Are you drunk or something to be calling me at least thirty times?" she asked.

She was at the warehouse terrace alone while Gaurav and Radhika were downstairs in their room talking.

"Where in the hell are you?! What are you doing?!" he demanded.

"Look, I can't tell you now, but the three of us are okay. And we can't talk for long." she said.

"Why not? Are you working with some bad guys or something?" he asked.

"Something like that. I got ourselves in this mess and we can't leave now." She said.

"You have to! The LOCKER needs to be sealed and Radhika's security must be disabled! Princi still doesn't know you're gone! But Nikhil won't shut his mouth for long! You have to come back!" he said.

"Oh shit!" she said.

"Can you understand how serious this is now?! Do something and come back!" he said.

"Arjun, I can't do that! Our bikes are with them! How can we escape?! And my leg…" she said, hesitant at the last word.

"Leg? What-what happened to your leg?!" he asked.

"I…I got shot." She said.

"What?! What the hell have you been doing?!" he exclaimed.

"That's the problem! Even if we escape, I can't run!" she said.

"Then what do I do?!" he asked.

"I'll call you back!" she said and cut the phone call.

"Simran- "he started but heard a beep.

Simran immediately rushed downstairs into their room and shut the door then bolted it.

"Radhika, Gaurav! We got a problem!" said Simran.

"What?!" they asked together and she told everything.

"Oh no…" said Gaurav while sitting down.

"What do we do?!" exclaimed Radhika.

"You go on! Go back to school!" said Simran.

"What?!" asked Gaurav.

"Even if I do, I won't reach until tomorrow! The Agents and Princi will get to know that we were missing all along!" she said.

"We can't escape these people, Simran." Said Gaurav.

"There's no other way. I'm wounded and I can't run. Gaurav might have a chance but he doesn't know the codes. You set this, Radhika. Only you know anyway." Said Simran.

"We can try to vouch for you when Aroop sees you gone." Said Gaurav.

"No, I can't leave you guys here and go back. What if something happens? And we have to go to Nepal tomorrow!" she said.

Just then, a knock came on their door and a guy opens it.

"We have to leave early tomorrow so come down for dinner right now." He said, waiting.

They gave a look to each other and went downstairs without a word. They quickly ate and went back to their room.

Back at school, Arjun walks back and forth in his room while Indira sat there waiting as well. just then, she received a text message from Nikhil. They gave a look at each other.

"They are here. They are on their way with Nikhil to the school. What do we do?!" asked Indira.

"She'll call. She has to call." He said.

"How are you so sure? What if she doesn't give a solution?" she asked.

"She will, okay?! I trust her!" he said.

"Trust her? YOU trust her, out of everybody?" she was surprised.

"Is that so hard to believe?" he asked.

"I don't know. You never trusted Nikhil. And now you trust her?" she asked.

"Yeah, I do and so does she." He said.

"She trusts you?!" Indira was perplexed at that.

"Believe what you like, I don't care." He said.

Chapter Eighteen –
On the Search...

"What the hell do we do, Simran?!" Radhika exclaimed.

The three of them were still awake after everybody went to sleep.

"Sshh! Do you want to wake everybody?" whispered Simran.

"I don't care anymore! We are so screwed! We still don't know what to do!" exclaimed Radhika.

"Now's your chance to go!" said Gaurav.

"I am not leaving!" she said.

"Well, then think of something else! The agents must be reaching by now!" said Gaurav.

Simran thought for a while.

"I was afraid this would happen! That's why I didn't want to go!" she said.

"Which is why you should go back." Said Gaurav.

"Okay, stop! I got it!" said Simran.

"What?" they asked.

"Radhika, I'm calling Arjun and you tell him how to disable the security system!" said Simran, while unlocking her phone.

"No way! You can't be serious! Arjun, out of all people?!" she asked.

"Does it look like I'm joking? Yes, Arjun!" she said, dialling his number.

"Gaurav, are you seeing this?" she asked.

"That's a great idea! He can do it!" – noticing Radhika's face – "Look, he changed, okay?" he said.

"No, he won't-"she started.

"I trust him, Radhika! I trust him!" said Simran, as the call kept connecting.

"Wh-what? Y-you really trust him?" she asked in disbelief.

"Hello?...Yeah Arjun, listen to me...yes, I got a plan. I'm giving the phone to Radhika and she will tell you how to disable the security...yes, you can do it...okay? Okay, Radhika!" she said, handing the phone over to her.

Radhika gives a look to her and to Gaurav then she takes the phone and gets up.

"Yeah, Arjun?" she said.

"Tell me. I can do this." He replied, still in his room with Indira.

"Okay, go to Simran's room and open her desk drawer. You will find two jumper cables in there." She said.

"Okay, hang on a second." He said and ran out of his room, down the stairs and up the stairs to Simran's room and entered.

Indira rushed inside behind him and they passed a confused and shocked Shreya to Simran's desk. Arjun opened the drawer and found the jumper cables.

"Okay, I got them. Now what?" asked Arjun.

"Go to the meeting room and connect the wires to the laptop in there." She instructed.

"Okay, hold on again." He said.

He left with the cables in his hands out the door and downstairs. Indira was about to follow him.

"What the hell was that all about?!" exclaimed Shreya.

"I promise I'll tell you later!" said Indira while running to catch up to Arjun.

They went to the meeting room and took out the laptop and connected the jumper cables in it.

"Okay, now?" he asked.

"Open the circuit board next to the LOCKER and connect the two cables in the two holes. Then a window will open." Said Radhika.

He did as he was told. A window had opened as she said. It was a blackish programming window.

"Okay, now what?" he asked.

"This is the tricky part. I don't know if you can do it. A few codes are required. It's basic C++ programming." She said.

"I don't know anything about that. But Indu's optional subject is computer science. Can that work?" he asked.

"Yes it can! Give the phone to her." She said.

Arjun did so and the girls continued to talk and Indira continued entering codes one by one. Finally she pressed enter and the hack in was completed. A few more instructions were given and the lasers turned off. Finally the security was disabled.

"Great work, Indu! We'll call soon." Said Radhika and cut the call.

She came back from a corner and sat down.

"Now, back to the real problem...Nepal! How can we go?! And secretly?! We'll be fired, Simran!" she said.

"But after finishing this business, we can go back to our lives! Nobody will kill us anymore!" said Simran.

"It's not only Prakash and his team...actually so far, they think you're dead. The one after us is that man who always makes every police station keep a picture of you. What do you plan on doing about that?" she asked.

"We'll solve that later, Radhika- "she started.

"No, you won't. You have to have a plan, Simran. A plan." She said.

"I have a plan. You never do." She said.

"Yes, I do. I don't interfere in dangerous matters. That's my plan!" she said.

"You are always taking the easy way out. That's a stupid plan!" said Simran, angrily.

"Both of you shut the hell up!" said Gaurav.

They became silent with anger.

"Look, it's Nepal. We're already so involved. We're just finishing what they have in store, get back to school as soon as possible and move on with class 12 and duty like nothing happened. So go to sleep now. I'm on first watch." He said, annoyed.

He got up and left them. He went and stood near the window. Radhika went and stood next to him after some time. Simran went to sleep.

"Nepal is another country, Gaurav..." said Radhika, softly.

"I know...I don't trust these people." He said.

"So what should we do? Simran might get better in another day. Till then, we can't escape. And when the time comes, we still can't." she said.

There was a silence between them.

"Hey, listen…" said Gaurav, putting his hand on her shoulder and gently squeezing it.

She turned and faced him. They looked at each other for a moment.

"Go sleep. I'll think of something." He said.

She sighed in disbelief but went to her bed and lied down.

As usual, she expects nothing from me…come on, Radhika!

Early in the morning, everybody's bags were packed and their bikes and jeeps were filled and ready. There were a total of three five-seater jeeps with five bikes, including the two bikes from school. Radhika and Gaurav were about to get on one bike when Aroop stopped them.

"Not to be rude but we'll be going really fast. You two sit with me and Simran in the jeep. Hand over the keys to them." He said and sat in the jeep opposite to Simran.

The two of them gave a look to the two guys and placed the bike keys in their hands. They turned and climbed aboard the back of the jeep. Gaurav sat next to Aroop and Radhika sat opposite to him next to Simran. They all started and reached the main highway in half an hour and drove smoothly in formation of the three jeeps in the middle while the bikes spread out.

"We will reach the border town of Raxaul in quite some time. We'll stop only once for lunch. We'll reach there late, rendezvous with our other team and stay the night. We'll leave for Kathmandu the next day." Said Aroop.

"Then?" asked Simran.

"Then what? We'll start searching." He said.

"But how will we start?" asked Gaurav.

"We'll obviously check the records from the truck depot first, right?" said Radhika and sighed disappointedly.

"Yeah, we'll ask around for him too." Said Aroop.

"Won't that take weeks?" asked Gaurav.

"Yeah…don't we have any other leads?" asked Simran.

"This is all I can find out. You guys better think." Said Aroop.

A few hours later, everybody stopped at a roadside food court and settled down at all the tables. Aroop sat with the others at another table while the three of them sat with two other guys at another table. Everybody was eating rice with a curry.

"Come on, can't there be any other way to find them? I have a feeling that we should go fast." Said Gaurav.

"Yeah, who knows what he might be doing collecting all that banned chemical." Said Simran.

"Hmm…I wonder if they know that we are coming for them." Said Radhika.

They all thought for a while eating.

"So what can sulphur mustard be made into?" asked Gaurav, suddenly.

"What's that have to do with finding them?" asked Radhika, sceptically.

"Just tell me, Simran." Said Gaurav, ignoring Radhika.

"Umm…let me find out and tell you. We can get there and find some wi-fi. Then I can find out." She replied.

"All right! Let's move out in five minutes!" Aroop announced. Everybody suddenly increased their eating pace and they were back on the road in five minutes. While they were sitting without a word in the jeep,

"So did you think of anything?" asked Aroop.

He looked at Gaurav, who shook his head. He then looked at Radhika who nodded in disappointment. He looked at Simran and he didn't say anything. She was thinking.

"Agent Khanna!" called out Aroop.

"I need internet." She said.

He chuckled.

"We'll get it at our destination." He said.

They were on the road for a few more hours till they reached the Indo-Nepal border in the town of Raxaul. They drove inside after stopping to show customs their details. In another twenty minutes inside the town, they reached a guest house and met the back-up team from HQ. There were at least twenty commandos. The head, who was at least middle aged, came and shook hands with Aroop.

"We have this entire building to stay in for the night. Tell your men to put their stuff in the rooms and relax for an hour. Then we'll have dinner." He said.

"You heard him." Said Aroop and everyone left.

As Simran was about to go upstairs, Aroop called out to her to stop. He came and whispered in her ear "#3456ramesh", winked and left with the head for discussions. She went on ahead with Radhika and Gaurav as fast as she could. They climbed two flights of stairs, went into a three-bed room and closed the door. Simran immediately took out her laptop and used that password.

Aha…wi-fi!

She continued typing and searching online. It took some time but finally she found the information.

"It can be used best as missiles for maximum impact." Said Simran.

Gaurav and Radhika were listening keenly. Nobody else was listening.

"Okay, more danger…we should just tell them and get out of here." Said Radhika.

"Not again…please stop deciding to go back home." Said Gaurav, annoyed.

"Well, don't you miss home?!" she asked.

"No, in fact, I feel at home here. You want to go back, go ahead." He said.

"Fine, I will!" she said, angrily while getting up.

"Just one problem!" said Simran, saying aloud. "They'll kill you."

She fell silent with anger. Gaurav turned his back to Radhika in ignorance, went and sat next to Simran on the bed to see her laptop screen. Just then, a knock came on the door with a man saying "Dinner in five minutes!" and leaving. Radhika gave one look of fury and turned to the door. She opened it, went out and slammed it shut with force.

"It is also used as munitions as aerial bombs, land mines, mortar rounds, artillery shells and rockets. The countermeasures against this were ineffective, since a soldier wearing a gas mask was not protected against absorbing it through his skin and being blistered. It remains persistent on the ground for days and weeks." Simran read out.

"Damn…lethal…search news if you can." Said Gaurav, requesting.

She nodded and searched. After typing some,

"In September 2015, a US official stated that the rebel militant group ISIS was manufacturing and using Sulphur mustard in Syria and Iraq. On November 8th, 2015, a report by the UN chemical weapon monitoring agency confirms that deadly sulphur mustard, commonly known as mustard gas, was used in an attack on a northern Syrian town in August." Said Simran, reading aloud.

"Hmm…" Gaurav wondered.

"What else do you want to know?" asked Simran.

"I wonder if ISIS sells it too." He said.

"Maybe not. They take credit for everything, don't they? They won't sell it to a five-member company." She said.

"All right…it's okay. We'll find out more later." He said.

They go down for dinner with everyone. They grab their plates of fried rice and eat. Radhika was eating alone at a corner. Simran and Gaurav made their way through the crowd of commandos eating towards Radhika, sit on either side of her and continued eating.

"So did you find anything?" asked Radhika.

They gave a look to each other and shook their heads in disappointment.

"Don't expect to be smarter than these people. They surely have better investigators, right?" said Radhika.

"Only the head and Aroop might be. Rest are commandos. They acknowledge our brains too. It doesn't hurt to try." Said Gaurav.

They all finished dinner. As everybody went upstairs into their rooms, Aroop called out to Radhika.

"You three be up and ready by 8:00am. We'll go to the truck depot tomorrow just when it opens." He said.

"Got it." she said and went upstairs.

She goes to their room and closes the door. She sees Simran stretching her leg for a while with Gaurav.

"Hey, Radhika, it's better!" said Gaurav, smiling.

"Good." She said.

"Go sleep, we'll take shifts now." Said Simran.

"Yeah, good night." She said and went to bed.

The next few days was spent in the city of Kathmandu at the truck depot by the head, Aroop and the trio. They were searching through logbooks, files, computer databases, etc., while the others spread out throughout the city in asking around. It took a lot of time and effort but there was no trace of Kapoor enterprises, let alone the numbers of the crates. One day, Simran and Aroop spend the entire day searching a room full of records.

"He never liked killing, you know?" he said.

"Who?" she asked.

"Your shooting teacher...he never liked killing."

"Did you ever meet him yourself?"

"We worked together many times...doing the same things."

"So was he one of Prakash's hit men like you?"

"No, I was hired later anyway. I only killed three LSS top 400. They were with him. And that boss of his."

"Wait a minute. He has someone to answer to? He's not the guy?"

"No, but he can lead us to the guy."

She was silent in surprise.

He's not the guy? Come on, get real. Why will he be controlled by someone else? This doesn't make sense because whatever he did till now, only he had the power to do. Who else would?

"I hope you know that we are in this because we want to know what he wants to do with that much lethal chemical. But we hope to not run into him." She said, clearly stating their intentions.

"If he is directly involved in whatever this is, then you can't avoid him..." he replied calmly.

"Understood. By the way, I hope he doesn't know I'm here." She warned.

"And I won't be telling him either..." he said, chuckling.

"And I should blindly believe you?" she asked, doubting him.

"I do owe him a favour for retiring. If it wasn't for him, I wouldn't have been promoted. But I won't." he said.

Retired? He retired? No way…

"Why?" she asked.

"Simple, I never liked him." He replied.

They continued searching but did not find anything that day.

In the truck depot the next day, Simran and Radhika access a list.

"Aroop, we got it." said Radhika.

He rushed over with a logbook he was checking.

"It's narrowed down to chemical storage crates of the medium box weights. At least 200 trucks in total. They loaded and left. Obviously these trucks left around the country. Not going out of the country." Said Radhika.

"Okay, here." - handing a piece of folded paper – "The three boxes are fully described in dimensions. Your search should be easier." He said.

They continued to search. After a few hours, the search was narrowed down to five trucks.

"Check the addresses from where they arrived from." Said Radhika.

"Chennai…okay, then Mumbai before that, then Jaipur… Delhi, Surat and Kolkata." Said Simran.

"Chennai is there but what about the other two? And it's not a guarantee that from Chennai that same crate arrived." Said Radhika.

"Hmm…" wondered Simran as she noted down the details.

They went back to their guest house in Kathmandu. Simran and Gaurav sat down at her laptop together. He had her paper on which the details of their last search. It had at least 30 trucks. One by one, Gaurav said the exact destination of all the trucks and Simran searched them. Some place was bound to get them curious. After a couple of hours of searching and noting down, the number of suspicious places came up were 19 in total all around Nepal. They went downstairs for dinner and were with Aroop and the head.

"So we've got a narrowed search but they still require time for checking out." Said Radhika.

"Why is that?" asked Aroop.

Gaurav handed the list to him and he briefly saw it.

"All these places are in different towns and cities. We need a few more days for this because we can only split up and search two to three towns or cities in one day and 19 of them…" said Aroop.

"We don't have any other way to go. No news is received from HQ yet so- "the head started but suddenly everybody was interrupted by one of the men coming with a cell phone.

"Aroop sir, it's for you." He said.

"Excuse me." Said Aroop and went with the phone outside. The head and the trio marked all the places in the list on a detailed map of the country. A while later, Aroop came back inside while putting his phone inside his pocket.

"Aroop, tomorrow we need to start searching with five teams, at least." Said the head.

"HQ tipped me on Prakash's current whereabouts. He is in Tehran, Iran to be exact. I and my guys have to leave right now." Said Aroop.

"What?!"

Everybody exclaimed in shock at this change of plan!

"Pack up, you three, if you want to get him." He said.

"Are you insane?" asked Simran.

"You can't be serious!" said Gaurav.

"I am dead serious. Prakash was seen there, checking into a hotel. I have to get there with my guys in the next 12 hours. So come on!" said Aroop.

"Aroop, they are just LSS! Be reasonable!" said the head.

"I don't have a choice! I need you all there!" he said.

"Forget it! We will not go!" said Radhika.

"Here, we can find something. If we don't then we'll just all go back home. You handle Prakash in Tehran." Said Gaurav.

"I don't want any arguments! We have to go!" said Aroop, sternly.

"Enough! I've had it with listening to you!" shouted Simran, angrily.

Everybody was silent.

"I know you need our help and so do we. But we can get more closure here. I thought you wanted to find the missing sulphur mustard but you are just after Prakash." She said.

Aroop silently listened.

"I know I owe you a favour but I can't go. I've found out enough about what you promised to tell. Please." She said.

He sighed.

"Fine, then stay here. I'm going. Give their bikes back to them." He said and turned around and leaving outside.

"Thank you." Said the head.

One guy came and handed over the keys to Gaurav and left. Simran went out after him to the cars.

"Aroop!" she called out.

He turned around and came to her. He walked straight up to Simran and stood a foot away looking fiercely down at her. She looked up at him fiercely as well.

"I may come back for you guys later. If you stay in one piece." He said.

"I think by the time you come back, we'll be at school. Safe and sound." She said.

"Don't be too sure on that." He said.

She gave a look of puzzlement.

"Remember one thing: my job was once to kill you. I won't do so, you know that. But there are more dangerous people like me. Irrespective of which side they are on, avoid them altogether. Quickly find your 'closure' and just go home." He said.

"Sorry that our priorities are different." She said.

"It's a good thing." He replied.

There was a pause.

"Whatever, I've got a lot of work to do. So I'll see you soon." He said and left.

After a few minutes, they all saw Aroop and his men catch a bus to the airport. The head was in charge now. But he called up the LSS Director to inform everything. Aroop had done a good job of not telling Vijayanti Rao but now it was inevitable. She was angry and she ordered the head to not allow the trio to set foot out of the hotel. He followed her instructions.

The next morning, everybody except the trio with a few other commandos, left the hotel towards the first couple of cities. Being considerate, the Head kept on mentioning their progress to them. The first couple of days passed with no luck. The places were abandoned.

On the third day, the trio were still in their hotel room. One commando was sitting outside in a chair and the opposite room had the rest four commandos resting, each about to get their shift to keep watch. Inside the room, the three of them could not sleep.

"I've had enough of the hotel food. It's not healthy to eat this stuff." Said Radhika, pushing a packet away.

"Then let's not eat this." Said Gaurav, taking and throwing the packet in the dustbin.

"Come on, guys." Simran said, whispering.

She was at the door of their room. She noticed the man outside fast asleep.

"Let's go eat something, then come back." Said Simran.

They sneak out of the room in the dark corridor and go downstairs out of the hotel. They walk for a while on the lighted street and search for a restaurant, bakery, café, etc. To their dismay, nothing to their interest was seen. After walking for some more time, the hotel was not to be seen. But they found a café and went inside. After some requesting, they were the last customers. They sat down at a table and started.

"So far they didn't find anything." Said Radhika.

"They just checked five towns and two cities. Many are left." Said Gaurav.

"The Director might come herself. We are so fired." Said Radhika.

They noticed Simran looking around, in thought.

"Hey, what happened?" asked Radhika.

"Ever since we reached Kathmandu, I was getting a feeling of being watched." She said, slowly.

"By whom? Any person from Kapoor enterprises?" asked Gaurav.

"I don't know…" she replied.

"The Director could've told your father. Oh my, what about him? What if he found you here?" asked Radhika.

"Who?" asked Gaurav.

"You don't know, Gaurav." She said.

"It's the guy who wants to kill us." Said Simran.

"He put the missing posters, right? That guy?" said Gaurav.

"Yeah, could be him too." Said Radhika.

Suddenly Simran got a call on her cell phone.

"Where the hell did-you- "some commando from the hotel called them and he sounded like he had difficulty in breathing.

"We just-what's wrong?" asked Simran, getting up.

Just then, the only other person in the restaurant, the cashier, got up and went into the kitchen. They noticed. They were alone in the place.

"Run away! They'll-they'll come! Get out of here! Go! Go now- "said the guy on the other line but suddenly the phone disconnected from his side.

"Who?! Hello?!" asked Simran but no reply came.

"Guys! We got to get out of here!" said Simran.

"But why?" asked Radhika, while getting up with Gaurav.

Suddenly the lights in the café turned off!

"Simran?!" called out Gaurav.

"Let's go! The commandos at the hotel were attacked!" said Simran.

"Shit!" they exclaimed.

"Sshh!" said Simran.

They fell silent and heard cars and footsteps around the building.

"They're here!" said Simran.

"But who? Prakash or him?" asked Radhika.

"Let's go first!" said Gaurav.

"AAHH!!!!"

CPSIA information can be obtained
at www.ICGtesting.com
Printed in the USA
BVHW042039100119
537595BV00007B/44/P